Return to Casa Grande

Michael Carlon

Also by Michael Carlon

Winning Streak

Uncorking a Murder

The Last Homily

All the F*cks I Cannot Give

Motel California

ISBN:0-9979839-2-2
ISBN-13:978-0-9979839-2-0

To Nicole, with whom I've been madly in love for the past 25 years.

CHAPTER ONE

Thanks for the Memories

Blaze Hazelwood lifted his hands up to his eyes and rubbed them, hoping that doing so would reduce the sting of the hangover that was setting in. It was sometime after 3 a.m. and the snoring coming from the other side of the bed reminded Blaze that he wasn't alone. He lifted up the sheets to get a glance at the woman he picked up earlier in the evening and shook his head knowing that, in his heyday, he could have done much better.

Knowing that sleep was not going to come back to him anytime soon, he got out of bed and walked over to his television and ejected a tape from his VCR. You read that right, a VCR; Blaze was an actor past his prime and stuck in the 1980s. He looked at the tape to confirm what was written on it and saw that the label read May 8, 1989. Satisfied, he popped the tape back into his VCR, rewound it, and hit play. He sat at the end of his bed to re-watch the last news story done about *Casa Grande*, the 1980s primetime soap opera that made him famous.

The picture was fuzzy, so Blaze had to adjust the

tracking on the machine. Once the level of clarity was passable, he saw the image of Kitty Carson, then a fifty-something reporter for a magazine devoted to soap operas, standing in front of the nightclub where the wrap party for *Casa Grande* was held twenty-five years prior.

"Greetings soap opera fans, Kitty Carson from 'The Soapdish' reporting. It's truly the end of an era—after 10 years on prime time, Casa Grande has closed its doors forever, leaving a hole in the hearts of the show's millions of devoted fans who will now have to turn elsewhere for their weekly dose of drama.

"*Casa Grande* was the very definition of the '80s soap opera. The show chronicled the lives of California winemakers the Thornridge family and featured every element synonymous with this golden age of prime-time soap—desire, power, jealousy, greed, murder, infighting and scandal. But network executives say viewer tastes are changing, so they're creating a drama geared toward younger adults for the coveted Monday at 10 p.m. time slot.

"Sources tell 'The Soapdish' that the new show, *LaMaze Academy*, will center on the lives of five teen girls attending a boarding school, who make a pact to all get pregnant during their junior year. Up-and-coming starlet Naomi Stevens is rumored to have a lead role.

"'Casa Grande has been a very successful show for the network, and it was a difficult decision to not renew the show for another season,' said network executive Geoffrey Crestwood. 'We wish the cast nothing but the best.'

"That's not what this reporter heard. Rumor has it that Crestwood's had it in for the show ever since the writers killed off the character Missy Thornridge, who was played by Crestwood's daughter Vanessa.

"But the Casa Grande body is not yet cold! How could I resist mentioning the revelations made last night? Spoiler alert for any of you who are going to watch it on your VHS players this evening: Madeline Thornridge, matriarch of the family, turned out to be having an affair with JR Solstice, 30 years her junior and the son of her nemesis, Sam Solstice of competing winemaker Global Wine Inc. We all knew she was seeing a mystery man for years, but even this imaginative entertainment reporter with a penchant for younger men didn't see that one coming.

"As if that weren't enough, we learned that Michael Thornridge arranged for the death of his sister Missy. His motive? He admitted to being in love with Kyle Dixon, the dashing young farmhand-turned-wine executive his late sister couldn't keep her hands off of.

"But perhaps the biggest bombshell of last night's series finale was learning that Missy Thornridge wasn't really dead after all—just as the handcuffs were about to be slapped on her brother Michael, Missy walked through the front door, and she was not alone. With her was a four-year-old boy, who we learned is the son of Barton Dixon, Kyle's father and the head caretaker of Casa Grande. Emotions changed on a dime for Kyle Dixon, who was visibly elated at the return of his lover yet instantaneously became furious to hear of her affair with his father. Then, in classic soap style, the lights flickered and a scream rang out! When the power came back on, we saw Kyle Dixon lying in a pool of blood, suffering from a stab wound but with no weapon to be found. The curtain closed on Casa Grande, leaving viewers wondering: Who stabbed Kyle Dixon?

"On their way into the after party, held at the ultra-trendy hot spot Vertigo in Hollywood, I spoke with fans on the street about their reactions to the series finale. Maria Vacodo had to be consoled by her sister Carol.

"It's like losing a friend," Maria said. "And I am just dying to know who stabbed Kyle!"

"I just can't believe it," said 22-year-old fan Catherine Rosdale. "I've been watching *Casa Grande* since its premiere in 1980 and have been hooked ever since. I want to have Blaze's baby!"

"She is referring, of course, to cast member Blaze Hazelwood, who played show hunk Kyle Dixon. Many women wore T-shirts that said Marry Me, Blaze. This reporter, old enough to be his mother, isn't too ashamed to admit she'd like a roll in the vineyard with the 20-year-old actor.

"You may recall the stir in West Germany earlier this year when Blaze was found to be having a secret affair with the mother of one-hit wonder Nena, of the song '99 Luftballons.' The Germans love Blaze, with his blond hair and blue eyes, and have caught a bad case of what they call Blaze Fieber, or Blaze Fever (auf Englisch). Apparently Blaze has a thing for older women; maybe there's a chance for me after all.

"I caught up with the cast members during the after-party to find out their plans for the future. Elizabeth Pierce, who played matriarch Madeline Thornridge, says she intends to take some time off."

"'Charles and I are going on an extended honeymoon,' Elizabeth said. 'He's always wanted to sail around the Greek islands, so that's what my current plan is, darling.'

"That's right—none other than Charles Pinkertoni, the Santa Barbara financier rumored to be connected with an Italian crime family. You didn't hear it here, lovelies, but the 30-year age difference between the two has left many wondering if Pinkertoni was looking for a beard to counter the rumors that he is a homosexual. If I go missing and my body is found at the bottom of the Pacific wearing cement shoes, you'll know I was right!

"Victor Tillmans, the actor who played head caretaker Barton Dixon, said he intends to buy a ranch in Simi Valley—a case of life imitating art.

"Danny Boy, who played Michael Thornridge, was living up to his Hollywood wild child image and had enjoyed one too many cocktails by the time I got to speak to him. Danny was slurring his words so badly I didn't even get a quote. I was able to make out that he'll be touring with his rock band Sinner's Swing this summer and may entertain offers for TV or movies after that. Oh Danny Boy, good luck with that.

"Vanessa Crestwood, who made her return to the show last night for its finale, says she is eager to show the world what she has to offer on the big screen—and that may mean revealing a bit of what her mama gave her.'

"'I've signed on to do a film with director Erick Shon," she admitted, dropping the name of the Hollywood director whose films border on soft-core pornography. "So I guess you will be seeing a lot more of me in the future.'

"And when it comes to series star Blaze Hazelwood, there will be no rest for the weary.

"'I want to show the world that there is more than one dimension to Blaze Hazelwood,' he said, 'so I am going to try my hand on the stage this summer.'

"This confirmed the rumors I'd heard earlier this week about Hazelwood getting the lead role of Marty McFly in *Back to the Future: The Musical.*

"All good things must come to an end, and such is the case with *Casa Grande.* One thing is for certain: prime time will never be the same, without the colorful cast and equally colorful storylines of *Casa Grande* to keep us entertained. As far as this reporter is concerned, there will never again be a show quite like it."

When the segment was over, Blaze pushed the stop button on his VCR and went back into his bed. He debated whether or not to wake up the girl, whose name he couldn't remember, but decided against it. Instead, he put his head on a pillow and his back toward the girl. He was asleep minutes later.

CHAPTER TWO

Blaze's Nightmare

Tension was running high at the Dolby Theatre in LA where the second annual Reality TV Awards were coming to a close and the final presenter of the evening was about to be announced by host Bret Michaels, the lead singer of '80s "hair band" Poison and former reality TV superstar. The most anticipated award of the night was about to be announced: the award for best new reality star.

"Ladies and gentlemen," Bret said, "to present the award for best new reality star, please welcome Ted McGinley."

The crowd applauded as Ted McGinley appeared onstage. McGinley was contractually obligated to appear on the awards show despite the fact that his own reality show, *Ted McGinley: Sitcom Killer*, had been canceled earlier that year. It made one question whether or not there would be a third annual Reality TV Awards, or if the McGinley curse would strike again.

"I am honored to present the final award of the evening. The nominees for best new reality star are..."

The theater went dark as large screens played clips of each show.

"Willie Aames for *Jesus in Charge.*" The audience saw a clip of Willie Aames throwing bibles at homeless people on LA's Skid Row while shouting, "Repent, repent, repent."

"William Katt for *Greatest American Heroes.*" The audience saw a clip of the actor interviewing "everyday Americans" about the good things they were doing in their local communities while sporting curly blond hair and the iconic red costume that made him a household name in the '80s.

"Emmanuel Lewis for *Forgetting Webster.*" The former child star was seen in a clip lying on a therapist's couch talking about how all he wanted to do was forget the sitcom character he played in the '80s.

"And Blaze Hazelwood for *Blaze of Glory.*" The audience saw 1980s heartthrob Blaze Hazelwood preparing for an audition by speaking lines to his reflection in a mirror. His blond hair was shorter than it was in the '80s, but his eyes were as blue as ever.

The house lights came back up, the monitor showing a four-way split screen with a feed of each nominee's face. McGinley opened the envelope and read: "And the award for best new reality star goes to...Blaze Hazelwood for *Blaze of Glory.*"

The crowd erupted in applause, and as Blaze walked onstage the orchestra played a classical rendition of David Hasselhoff's "Looking for Freedom." Blaze accepted the award from McGinley and then turned his attention to the crowd.

"First, I would like to thank the members of the Reality

Show Academy for nominating me for this award. My competition was formidable and I have a great deal of respect for my fellow nominees. Honestly, I have not felt this excited since a cool November evening 25 years ago when I found myself in West Berlin. When the crowds on the east side of the Berlin Wall pushed their way through to the west I remember thinking to myself it was the most intense one-sided game of Red Rover I had ever seen."

Blaze paused to allow the crowd a moment to laugh, but no one did. A little shaken, he cleared his throat and continued: "In the 25 years since that cool November night I've learned one thing..." Blaze paused and looked at the crowd, then said, "Who the fuck am I trying to kid?" The crowd gasped at his use of profanity—surely Blaze must have known this was being broadcast live. "I am better than this. What I said about my competition being formidable, that was bullshit. I'm the only star in this room! You can take this meaningless piece of crap award and shove it up your bums."

Blaze then extended his right arm and dropped his award, which broke in three pieces, and walked offstage shouting "Reality TV is bullshit" as the orchestra began to play.

"Blaze, Blaze!" a beautiful brunette said while shaking the sleeping man beside her violently. "Wake up, you're talking in your sleep."

Blaze turned over and looked at the woman who was shaking him. "What is your name again, luv?" Blaze said the word luv with a British accent. While Blaze's hometown of Little Falls in upstate New York was far away from England, he had developed an affectation of speaking with a British accent from time to time. Even though they only met once over two decades ago, Blaze considered Madonna a close friend and saw how her developing a similar affectation helped keep her relevant after almost four decades in show business. Blaze thought that if it worked for Madge, it could also work for him.

The "luv" in bed next to Blaze was a twenty-two-year-old waitress named Betty who had waited on Blaze earlier that evening. Even though he wasn't a household name anymore, his boyish good looks coupled with his blond hair and piercing blue eyes along with his charm kept him a player in the seduction game.

"Betty, you asshole! You were talking in your sleep."

"What was I saying, Betty, luv?"

Betty looked at Blaze softly and her demeanor changed; she softened her tone. "You kept mumbling that reality TV is bullshit."

"Of course it is, luv," Blaze replied. "I was dreaming that I won the award for best new reality TV star. I got angry and stormed offstage."

"Wow, does that mean I just had sex with an award-winning actor?"

"Only in my dreams, luv."

"Well, Mr. Hotshot," Betty said, sliding her hand down his chest, "why don't we celebrate your big award?"

"I won't argue with that, luv."

CHAPTER THREE

Meet T-Bang

"I can't believe I have to meet with a guy named T-Bang," Allison Hart said to Lucy Nichols, one of her production assistants. At 30, Allison was the quintessential up-and-comer at Universal Products Company, or UPC for short. The multinational conglomerate, which made everything from bath soap to TVs and was even rumored to dabble in the defense sector, had been struggling in recent years to identify a new advertising model that worked. The fragmentation of the media universe, and viewers "zapping" their way through commercials, left corporations struggling to find ways to reach buyers. That was why UPC had hired Allison.

Allison had seen the popularity of reality television skyrocket just as network advertising revenue started to fall. In her final year at Harvard Business School, she'd made the case that consumer product companies should abandon traditional TV advertising altogether and focus instead on product placement in reality TV shows. Then Allison went a step further, arguing that in order to control the conversation, consumer goods companies should create their own programming, since owning the show means owning placement—an advertising method modeled on the early days of radio and television, when companies such as Procter & Gamble created the shows they sponsored. It was this model that had created the soap opera.

But Allison isn't all brains; in fact, she always felt as if her classic good looks were a detriment to her. At five feet eleven inches, she was taller than most of the girls she went to school with. Her long blond hair and athletic physique also caused the heads of both men and women to turn whenever she walked by. Because of this, Allison felt as if she had to work three times as hard as anyone else in order to be taken seriously.

Through her connections at Harvard, she was able to present her ideas on marketing to Brandon Master, the chief executive officer of UPC. Master hired her on the spot and immediately made an offer to buy Pocket Box, the fledgling online network dedicated to creating custom programming for the 18-to-24-year-old market. Pocket Box would be their distribution vehicle for the programming ideas Allison had, and this is where T-Bang came in.

"He can be an ass, but he's kind of charming in a low-rent kind of way," Lucy said to her boss. "He's actually kind of cute."

It's true; behind the multiple gold chains and the beard that looked as if it could have been drawn with a fine-tipped pencil, T-Bang was not what most women would consider ugly. His brown hair was cut very close to his scalp, allowing admirers to see his perfectly shaped head—

his mother chose to give birth by C-section for fear of her narrow birth canal causing what was considered an above-average-sized head to take on a cone shape immediately after birth. But the pièce de résistance was the cleft on his chin—a cleft so pronounced that he would invite women to sip whatever it was they were drinking right from his "chimple."

"Cute or not, I never dreamed I would actually have to interact with talent, and I use that term very loosely," Allison replied. "I have an MBA from Harvard and now I have to spend my afternoon buttering up to someone named T-Bang? I guess if we have learned anything from the Kardashians it is that you no longer have to have talent in order to be famous."

Lucy disagreed with her boss on that point; she was secretly a reality TV junkie and knew the comings and goings of the Kardashians, Tori Spelling, and even the Duggars. Additionally, she was annoyed that her boss dropped the Harvard line again; why do people who went to Harvard always have to mention that they went to Harvard?

Thaddeus Stevens, a.k.a. T-Bang, was the 24-year-old son of '90s TV star Naomi Stevens and her life partner, Eric Peters, a high-profile entertainment attorney. When Thaddeus was conceived during the filming of *LaMaze Academy*, the breakout hit that made Naomi a household name in the '90s, the show's producers decided to let Naomi raise him on set. Since the program focused on a group of girls who had made a pact to get pregnant, the writers had little difficulty writing Thaddeus into the show. Over the years, audiences fell in love with his character, Michael Allen.

Deciding at age 18 to break out of his "goody-goody" image, Thaddeus adopted the name T-Bang. He now could be found running wild in Hollywood with his crew of former prep-school kids turned wannabe thugs. His erratic behavior at Hollywood's nightspots, coupled with the long list of young female celebrities he was rumored to have bedded, earned the attention of a UPC brand manager, who thought T-Bang would be a great vehicle to promote the company's Lust brand of products—a cross-category line targeting the personal care needs of teenage boys, including shaving cream, body spray, and body wash. Now Allison had to pitch a "celebreality" show she had crafted around T-Bang and his "crew"—and do whatever was needed to get him to sign.

Allison's attention was momentarily diverted from Lucy when her instant messaging application started to blink. It was Marios, her personal assistant, letting her know that T-Bang had arrived, along with two members of his entourage. Allison replied to keep them entertained for 15 minutes before showing them to her office. She wanted to be the one in control of this meeting and didn't want to look too eager.

\#

T-Bang and his merry band of misfits took their seats in the waiting room outside Allison's office. While waiting for his boss to come out of her office, Marios was privy to one of the most inane conversations he'd ever heard.

"That bitch gonna be like all over the T-Bang, man, know mean?" one of them said.

"Yo yo yo, check it out, T-Bang gonna filet that like the Gorton's mothafuckin' fisherman," replied another. This conversation was accentuated with grunts of "aw snap" and fist bumps.

It took all his strength for Marios not to burst out into laughter at this exchange. Sitting before him were three of the whitest boys he had ever seen. Beneath the flat-brimmed ball caps, the gold chains, the fake gold teeth, the rings, the vintage Run DMC T-shirts, and the baggy pants worn below the waist, Marios saw three young men of privilege desperately trying to live in a world they clearly knew nothing about.

T-Bang was too busy composing a tweet to respond to his friends. T-Bang saw it as his responsibility to keep his over one million Twitter followers in the know about the comings and goings of his life. His followers knew what he ate for breakfast, lunch, and dinner every day. They knew when he was drunk and when he was horny. They always knew when he was bored, since that was when he tended to tweet the most. The best he could offer to them at that moment was "At UPC/Pocket Box to hear a pitch. Pocket Box—like a sex toy." Within seconds of sending that tweet, T-Bang had multiple offers from women offering their box for his pleasure.

His attention was diverted from his mobile phone when one of his friends asked about the party they were planning for his 25th birthday. "Yo, T, you think your parents will let us host your 25 throwdown at their place in Malibu next month? I got Big Kenny and Road Dawg waiting in the wings." Big Kenny and Road Dawg were the two hottest DJs in LA. "Your parents' place is off the hizzie."

"My moms hasn't given me a straight answer yet, yo. I think she's still bent that we tag-teamed that ho." Earlier that week, Naomi had caught her best friend and former

LaMaze Academy co-star Jenna Talia in bed with her son and his friend Freddy. Jenna had tried to explain that the boys were just helping her through a hard time, but Naomi was outraged.

"Don't worry, T," his friend replied. "It'll all blow over, just like it always does."

Marios realized he was paying too close attention to this conversation when his phone started to ring. His angry boss asked, "Didn't you see my instant message? I'm ready to see him now, please show him in." Marios apologized to her and then announced to T-Bang that Allison was ready for him.

"Want us to go in there with you, T?" his friend Freddy asked.

"I gots this one, boyz," T-Bang proclaimed. "If the meeting takes more than 10 minutes, you know I be knockin' some boots, ohh." At that, fist bumps were followed by chest bumps, and T-Bang walked into Allison's office.

#

Allison waited a moment after T-Bang sat down before sitting down herself. "Thank you for coming in, Thaddeus."

The use of his first name annoyed him. "The name is T-Bang, the only one who calls me Thaddeus is my moms."

"Do you have more than one mother?" Allison asked.

"Nah, it's like, I say moms when I really mean mom. It's just the way I speak. Dat okay wif you?"

"Of course," Allison said disdainfully. "You have quite the reputation, Mr. T-Bang. You've been involved in multiple altercations in Hollywood clubs, yet you never wind up in the police blotter."

T-Bang smiled. "It pays to have a lawyer in the family." He was referring to his father.

"You're constantly hired by club promoters to attend events. When you do, there are lines out the door of people wanting to meet you."

"Being bad pays off, I guess."

"It would certainly appear that way. Tell me, T-Bang, how would you like to make some real green?" Allison knew to build rapport by adjusting her speech; she even started to subtly mirror T-Bang's movements. When he blinked, she blinked. When he crossed his arms, she crossed her arms, and when he leaned in, she leaned in. She would know that she had him when he started to mimic her body language.

"Yo—T-Bang is all about the Benjamins," he replied, referencing the founding father whose image is on the one-hundred-dollar bill. "How you gonna make it rain for me is what I wants to know."

"We here at UPC think your life is fascinating. As such, we have crafted a show around it. All aspects of your life will be captured and streamed to Pocket Box subscribers."

"Yo, stop right there. T-Bang don't wants a camera crew following him around. It just ain't natural, you feel me?"

"That's the beauty of modern technology. We will actually plant small pinhole cameras on you and the members of your crew. No one will see them. They will communicate by Bluetooth to a smartphone that we will give you. The video will then be beamed back to our servers, then streamed to the Pocket Box community."

"Wait, so everything we do will be shared? That's not

gonna fly—what abouts when I wants to get with a shorty?"

Allison found T-Bang's derogatory attitude toward women—and everything else about him—extremely offensive. But she bit her tongue; the deal was more important than her opinion on what constitutes acceptable standards of behavior.

"We thought of that," Allison explained. "If there's ever a situation that you don't want to record, whether it be an intimate situation or a situation where legality may be in question, all you have to do is click a kill switch on the smartphone. That will immediately stop the broadcast until you turn it back on."

"Sounds dope. But you still haven't told me how you gonna make it rain money for T-Bang." This was the second time T-Bang had spoken of himself in the third person.

She uncrossed her arms and noticed he did the same. She knew it was time to reel him in.

"All network television is sponsored by advertisers and this will be no different."

T-Bang interrupted her, "Wait, you tellin' me there's gonna be commercials on my show?"

"No, not exactly. We can't have commercials, because the idea of the show is that it is your life unfolding in real time. Real life doesn't have commercial breaks. What we intend to do is have advertisers give you products to use. We simply ask that you use them at some point each day."

T-Bang got up abruptly and exclaimed, "T-Bang ain't no sellout."

Allison had expected this reaction from her guest. "You'll be paid $20,000 a week and be given a contract for 52 weeks, which we will honor even if your show gets canceled."

T-Bang couldn't hide his Cheshire Cat grin as he sat back down.

"What do you say to that, Mr. T-Bang?"

"There's only one thing to say," T-Bang said. "Bling it on, baby."

And that's how *Bling It On Featuring T-Bang* became the first ever celebreality show produced by Allison Hart of UPC and streamed from Pocket Box.

CHAPTER FOUR

Blaze Gets Therapy

Blaze was lying on the leather couch in his agent's office as if he were in a therapy session. He was wearing a pastel shirt, white pants and loafers without socks as if it were the mid 1980s and he was about to go on an audition for *Miami Vice*. Stanley, Blaze's agent, put down the current issue of *Variety* he was thumbing through and let out a large sigh. "Can you please stop doing that?"

"Doing what?" Blaze was oblivious to the fact that he was throwing a blue racquetball up in the air and catching it while waiting for his agent to finish the article he was reading.

"Throwing that damn ball up in the air! Why are you here anyway?"

Blaze did not have an appointment to meet with his agent; he popped in unannounced that afternoon.

"You need to get me back on TV, Stanley! Blaze Hazelwood was meant to be seen, not lend his voice to fucking cartoons and video games." One of Blaze's bad habits, aside from his British affectation, was referring to himself in the third person.

In the years since *Casa Grande* went off the air, Blaze regularly found work doing voiceovers, and he longed for the days of being on screen again.

"Speaking of which," Stanley said while not bothering to look up from the pages of the magazine he was reading, "how did that voiceover work go last week?"

Blaze replied in an agitated manner, "When you told me I would be voicing a character named Winged Foot in a video game called *Flight of Fancy*, I assumed it would be something teenage boys would play. It turns out, I was voicing a fucking pink pony in a game designed for grade-school girls! Do you know what my character's catchphrase was? Do you?"

"Enlighten me," Stanley replied.

"We have pony power!" Blaze said animatedly while making a throat-slashing gesture with his finger. "And don't get me started on that fucking voice director, the worst!"

"Did the check clear?" Stanley asked wryly.

"You should know; your percentage was deducted!"

"Hey, I gotta eat, too."

Blaze sat up on the couch. "Well you don't seem to be missing too many meals there, Stanley old boy."

"Hey, all I am saying is that unlike your former co-stars, you are making a very good living."

"I am not low on money, Stanley, I am low on relevance. It used to be I could walk into a bar and have any woman I wanted. Do you want to see what I went home with last night?"

"Not particularly, but I have a feeling you are going to show me anyway."

Blaze got up from the couch, removed his phone from his pocket, and found a picture that he took of his overnight guest from the night before.

Stanley picked up the phone and said, "Are you sure that's a woman?"

"Yes, but there were times when I had my doubts."

"Look, my heart goes out to you, Blazey boy, but from where I am sitting, you have it really good. Do you remember Elizabeth Pierce?"

"Remember? I would kill to forget her! That drunken witch made my life miserable on the set of *Casa Grande*. I always imagined her throwing wire hangers at homeless people just for the fun of it."

"Well, the only work I could get for her in the past year was a job on an infomercial pitching reverse mortgages. She can barely pay her bills."

"Karma is a bitch!"

"How about Vanessa Crestwood, do you remember her?"

"I think I was the only one on the show that she didn't screw. How could I forget her?"

"Tune in to the TV Shopping Network later this today and you will see her pitching some new kind of toy. She also hasn't worked in years."

"Hey, whatever happened to Danny Boy? He and I used to party hearty together back in the day."

"Danny, now there's a sad case!"

"Don't tell me he died!" Blaze said.

"Worse, he found God and became a priest. He was assigned to a parish up in Agoura Hills and completely turned his life around. Clean and sober for about 10 years now. It's a damn shame. Do you remember Victor?"

"Good old Victor! That man taught me everything I know about picking up women. Please don't tell me he's a priest, too."

"He's loopier than a noose in a spaghetti western. Strangest thing, a few years back he started this habit of riding his horse naked through the streets of Simi Valley, kind of like a male version of Lady Godiva. He's now living in some retirement home up in Westlake Village."

"I guess when you put it like that, I'm not doing so bad, am I?"

"Look, I'll do what I can to get you in front of the camera, but the only thing coming across my desk for you these days is rea…"

Blaze cut Stanley off before he could finish his sentence.

"So help me God, if the words reality TV come out of your mouth I will stick a fork into your heart."

"Look, I know how you feel about it, but that's where the opportunities are these days."

Blaze looked at his watch and then looked concerned. "Shit!"

"What's the matter?"

"I just remembered, I have to be in Westwood in two hours."

"That's ten miles away, you'll never make it. What's in Westwood anyway?"

There were few places where you could not traverse ten miles in two hours; LA at rush hour was one of them.

"Do you mind if I change in your bathroom?"

"Go right ahead, but you didn't answer my question. What is in Westwood?"

Blaze walked to the bathroom in Stanley's office and closed the door. "I got a call this morning about participating in a focus group at 6 p.m. I am supposed to play a teacher"

Stanley rolled his eyes; play was the wrong word.

"You still do those things?"

Blaze came out of the bathroom wearing a button-down shirt, khaki pants, and a tie. Capping off his transformation into a teacher were a wig and glasses.

"How many times do I have to tell you, they are a great way to adapt different personas and build my acting chops."

"You know, you could be just like any other actor and take acting lessons or workshops?"

"But that's the thing, luv," Blaze said with his British affectation. "I am not just any other actor. I am Blaze fucking Hazelwood!"

CHAPTER FIVE

An Aging Starlet

Elizabeth Pierce woke up late in the afternoon with a screaming headache. Once a glamorous starlet who graced both the big and small screen, Elizabeth was now just another 70-year-old woman with a Hollywood past and a drinking problem. Though her hair had turned gray a long time ago, she attempted to defy her age, and save what little money she had left, by coloring it at home. Actresses are not hairdressers—this was made evident by the bright shade of orange adorning Elizabeth's head. She looked more like the comedian Carrot Top than Lucille Ball, whom she was attempting to resemble. At least I still have Charles, she thought to herself. She moved her hand over to the right side of the bed and found it empty.

He must be downstairs, she thought to herself. Elizabeth managed to sit up, albeit not without feeling queasy, and put on the pair of pink slippers that she always kept at the foot of her bed. She checked the tightness of her bathrobe's belt—at 70 one couldn't be too careful; she wouldn't want to inadvertently flash "the girls" to an unsuspecting house guest.

Elizabeth made her way downstairs, but there was no sign of Charles in the kitchen. As she started the coffee she heard slurping sounds coming from the mudroom and found Charles on all fours drinking water out of a bowl on the floor.

"Who's a good boy? Who's Mommy's little angel?"

Charles stopped what he was doing, looked in Elizabeth's direction, and then recommenced his morning drink. "Is it too much for you to give me a kiss on my birthday?" Elizabeth sneered at her five-year-old dachshund, a pet with a disposition as equally nasty as that of its owner. He was named Charles, like each of his four predecessors, because when her husband Charles left her for another man, Elizabeth swore off all men, declaring them all dogs. Since then she had sought only four-legged companions.

When the coffee was ready, Elizabeth sat down at her table with the newspaper. She preferred to read the news from the day before, as she had an irrational fear of reading her own obituary in that day's paper. She once explained this to her therapist, who asked her why she thought she would be able to read the paper if she were dead. Elizabeth fired him on the spot, arguing, "That's what I'm paying you to help me figure out."

Life had not been easy for Elizabeth since the end of *Casa Grande*, the TV drama that had marked her last starring role. Shortly after the show ended, so did her marriage—and her husband, Charles, was granted a hefty settlement. Pierce vs. Pinkertoni marked the first time a man was granted half of a woman's fortune during a divorce settlement. There'd been gossip that the fix was in from the beginning, that Charles's organized-crime connections blackmailed the judge to settle in his favor. Whatever the reason, Elizabeth didn't work at all after *Casa Grande*, and she burned through her savings quickly. She now lived in a small condominium in Culver City, just around the corner from the soundstages that had made her famous.

After reading the paper, she turned her attention to the stack of mail piled on her counter. Thumbing through it, she found nothing but bills, collection notices, and a letter from the bank notifying her that if she did not pay $50,000 in overdue mortgage payments, she would be evicted from her home in one month.

Charles walked over to her, leaving a trail of his drool from his dog bowl. Sensing she was distraught, he put his head in her lap. Scratching him behind the ears, Elizabeth muttered, "What are we going to do, Charlie, my boy? If only I could return to Casa Grande everything would be okay." She then proceeded with her other morning ritual: drowning her sorrows with her trusty old friend Johnny Walker.

CHAPTER SIX

The Prodigal Son of Casa Grande

Daniel Maieye's mouth was dry—a symptom not of the drug habit he had kicked years ago but of his fear of public speaking. He was about to address a room full of people and he always got nervous when performing "live." He still had the rugged good looks that helped him to stardom all those years ago, although there was now a significant amount of gray in his previously dark hair, around the temples. When not dressed in his clerical garb, he was often mistaken for Richard Grieco, which was ironic considering that Daniel, back when he was known as Danny Boy, was up for the role of Michael Corben in 1991's *If Looks Could Kill*. The role went to Grieco after a strung-out Danny Maieye showed up shitfaced to a meeting with the film's producers.

Daniel began by showing his gratitude to those who had gathered that morning. "I'd like to thank you for the warm welcome. I know there are a few of you who are skeptical about my being here, and your skepticism is understandable; it's not every day someone from my former profession enters this one." He took a minute to gesture around the room and even point toward the clothes he is wearing. "But let me assure you, my heart is pure, as are my intentions. In today's gospel we heard the familiar story of the prodigal son—the young man who asked his father for an advance on his inheritance so he could go live the high life, only to spend it all unwisely, on material items and pursuits of the flesh. We heard how this once-rich man became a slave to another and was only given the leftover scraps that were given to the pigs. This is such a powerful story, because there is someone for all of us to identify with. Some identify with the brother, who is jealous that his father has shown mercy on the other son. Some identify with the father, who out of the goodness of his heart welcomes his son back with open arms. I, however, identify most with the prodigal son himself."

Formerly one of Hollywood's bad boys, Danny Boy turned his life around ten years ago after hitting rock bottom following a three-day partying binge across California, Arizona, and Nevada. He had woken up in a hotel room, not knowing where he was and surrounded by chickens. Also in the room were Vanessa Crestwood, his former *Casa Grande* co-star, and six other people, all of whom were naked.

Danny was able to find his clothes, leave the room, and make it to the elevator. After the doors opened in the lobby, he heard the unmistakable ringing and dinging of a casino and concluded he was in Vegas. Feeling suddenly queasy, Danny broke out in a cold sweat when he saw that the men's room was all the way across the lobby. Knowing he would never make it, he headed instead toward the hotel fountain in the middle of the lobby, just 25 feet away from the elevator.

This being Vegas, the fountain wasn't just any old fountain—its jets were synchronized to music. When Danny arrived in the lobby, the fountain was putting on a "show" to "Your Body Is a Wonderland" by John Mayer, a musical choice that didn't help his situation. Danny started retching, with just five feet to go before reaching the fountain, and he started to sprint but tripped on his own shoelaces and hit his head on its base, vomiting as he did. When he managed to stand up, everyone in the lobby witnessed the disheveled man, covered in vomit, fall head-first into the fountain, while John Mayer sang about wanting to boff the brains out of some teenage girl.

As luck would have it, a registered nurse turned nun named Sister Mary Patrick was playing the slots in the lobby, and she dashed over to Danny before hotel security could get to him. She jumped into the fountain to pick him up and keep him from drowning.

Danny opened his eyes and saw his savior, a 50-year-old woman wearing a nun's habit, holding his head gently in her hands. Hotel security arrived, and Sister Mary Patrick requested a first-aid kit and a can of Coca-Cola. While waiting to receive the requested supplies, Sister Mary Patrick asked some basic questions, to gauge the level of trauma to Danny's head. He was able to state his name, address, and age; the only thing he couldn't answer was what he was doing in Vegas. Danny would never forget the words of his savior: "You have to change your life or else you will die."

From that day forward, he quit partying, severed ties with his old friends, started going by his birth name of

Daniel Maieye and turned his life over to the Church. While ashamed of his past, he felt as if he could use his experience to help others. He had written today's homily, in fact, with his own past in mind. "So it is serendipitous that my first mass at a new parish has the parable of the prodigal son as its gospel. I left my family and faith many years ago only to lead a life full of excess; I'm sure more than one of you prayed to Our Lady of Google when you heard I was assigned to your parish. Unfortunately, I can assure you that most of what you read is actually true! That said, I do believe that hearts can change and, just like the prodigal son, I believe that forgiveness is available for all those who seek it. I do have one favor to ask of you, as you pray for your loved ones tonight—please say a prayer for me as well, and I promise to do the same for all of you. May God bless you all."

Rarely does a homily in a Catholic church move a crowd to applause, but that is exactly what happened that Sunday morning at Our Lady of the Hills Catholic Church in Agoura Hills, California; even the skeptics were clapping. There was one woman, though, who kept her hands firmly folded across her chest; it was Vanessa Crestwood's first time in a church since she made her own confirmation in the ninth grade, and while the other congregants were feeling a sense of joy and excitement for their new pastor, she felt nothing but rage.

CHAPTER SEVEN

Vanessa Gets Buzzed

Vanessa Crestwood was nervous. It had been years since she'd been on a screen of any size, and she hoped that today's performance on the TV Shopping Network would thrust her back into the limelight.

After *Casa Grande*, Vanessa starred in a movie called *Fallen Angels*, about a group of four all-American girls from the Midwest trying to make it in Hollywood. Given his proclivity toward sexually explicit movies, director Erick Shon couldn't turn down the chance to show the girls' traditional Midwestern values erode as each begin to trade sexual favors for casting consideration. By the middle of the film, they are all involved in hardcore pornography. By the end, three of the four are dead. The final scene shows Vanessa Crestwood's character, now known as Misty Mountain, in front of the graves of her three fallen friends; she vows to get out of the business, but not before giving oral sex to a movie producer behind her friends' gravestones.

The movie was panned by critics and moviegoers alike;

one critic wrote, "*Fallen Angels* makes *Showgirls* look like *The Godfather*." Vanessa couldn't get arrested after that, never mind land an audition. It wasn't that she was no longer good-looking; her shoulder-length brunette hair, creamy complexion, and well-toned physique would be an asset to anyone looking to grace the small or big screen. Instead what held her back was her reputation of being difficult to work with; one former co-star claimed that she looked just like Shannon Doherty without the gap in her teeth but with twice the attitude problem.

But today was going to be different! Today, Vanessa was going to start a new chapter in her life—celebrity pitchwoman. Vanessa struck a deal with an adult toy company to be the pitchwoman for the Vibratoe, a personal massager shaped like a toe. Rather than a salary, she was to be paid a 10 percent commission for every product sold. With a retail price of $49.99, if she was able to move a million units through TVSN, she would walk away with almost $5 million. Yes, today was the proverbial first day of the rest of her life. A production assistant told Vanessa that she was up next and Vanessa took a deep breath.

The person before her was a toymaker pitching a line of action figures called Martyrs of the New Testament. There was John the Baptist, in a beard and loincloth, whose head was removable. Accompanying him was a small silver platter to hold the head, once detached. St. Stephen came with plastic rocks. St. Thomas came with a big question mark on his tunic. Vanessa was filled with hope as the products sold out during the ten-minute segment. The toymaker practically danced off the set and the production assistant told Vanessa it was time for her to take his place.

Walking on the soundstage, Vanessa was greeted by the host, Piper Jasmin. Thirty seconds later Piper looked into the camera and said, "Hello, we are back and we have a very special guest with us right now. Some of you may remember Vanessa Crestwood from her starring role in the '80s soap opera *Casa Grande*. Well, today she is here to pitch an exciting new product. What do you have for us, Vanessa?"

"Thank you, Piper. I'm very excited to be here. Today I want to talk to you all about a revolutionary new product that will empower today's modern female road warriors to travel with ease."

"Sounds interesting," Piper said. "What is this miracle product?"

"First off, let me tell you a story about something that happened to a friend of mine while going through airport security. She put her purse through the scanner, but she had forgotten to take her laptop out. This triggered the TSA agent to manually comb through her entire bag—and then the most embarrassing thing happened: the TSA agent came across my friend's vibrator, pulled it out of her bag, and asked her what it was. She was completely mortified."

Not as mortified as Piper Jasmin. Her guest had just told a story about a vibrator on live TV, in the middle of the day. Before she could interrupt, Vanessa continued.

"So I am here today to talk to you about this little lifesaver: the Vibratoe." Vanessa then took out what appeared to be a prosthetic big toe, complete with red nail polish. "This looks just like any other toe, but underneath the nail bed is a small three-way switch. Move it to the right for a setting entitled 'tiptoe,' designed specifically for those girls who want to ease into their experience. One more slide to the right and you have 'tic, tac, toe.' This is a random game-like setting and it's very unpredictable, perfect for a little tease. The third and final setting is called 'toegasm' and is guaranteed to have you biting your lip within two minutes. Ladies, you can pack this in your bag without anyone knowing your little secret."

The entire soundstage became so quiet you could hear a pin drop and, for once in her life, Piper Jasmin was at a loss for words. The counter showing how many people had either called to order the product or purchased it online remained in the single digits.

Vanessa, clearly uncomfortable with the silence but oblivious to the awkwardness of the situation, said, "I see the phones have lit up, Piper, why don't we go to the phones and take some calls?"

Before Piper could finish saying, "I'm not so sure that's such a good idea," Vanessa reached over and grabbed the mouse attached to the computer in front of Piper and, clicking on the first caller, said, "Thanks for calling, you are on with Vanessa and Piper."

"How in the hell can you follow a guy selling religious action figures with this crazy piece of..." Before he got his last word out, Vanessa clicked the mouse to move on to the next caller.

"Hi, you're on with Vanessa."

"Hi, Vanessa, I've been a big fan of yours for a long time. I feel like I know you."

"Aww, that's so sweet, what's your name, baby?"

All viewers heard next was the caller screaming "Babba-booey, babba-booey" into the telephone.

"Well, they say the third time is a charm," Vanessa said. "Caller, you are on with Vanessa."

"Yeah, Vanessa, my name is Maria and I'm a TSA agent. While I can understand your friend being embarrassed about having her vibrator found in her carry-on, what do you think she would say if the TSA agent asked her what she was doing with a prosthetic toe in her bag? Doesn't that seem a bit odd to you?"

Piper finally recovered her ability to speak. "Well, caller, you have just asked the question that has been on all of our minds since this segment began. I think now is a good time to take a break."

Vanessa looked defeated once the cameras were turned off. She glanced at the counter and saw that only 69 Vibratoes had been sold, grossing her a whopping $344.93. After taxes she would be lucky to net $240. At this point she felt as if she had only one option available to her: go crawling back to her father on her hands and knees and ask for a loan. It's not as if he couldn't afford it. Geoffrey Crestwood was a millionaire many times over having made his fortune running the network that aired *Casa Grande*. A devout Christian, her father made it clear that if she chose to do soft-core adult films, she would be cut off from his wealth. She knew her father would help her but only if she were willing to admit that she made a mistake; and that was something she was loath to do.

CHAPTER EIGHT
Victor Victoria

The sun was shining brightly through Victor Tillmans' window, and while this would cheer up your average human being, it only served to annoy Victor, who had been in the same room at the Shady Acres retirement home for the past 10 years.

After Casa Grande ended, Victor followed through with his dream of buying a ranch in Simi Valley, California. He had hundreds of acres, where he let his dozens of horses graze freely. The people of the town loved having a celebrity in their midst—until Victor's presence became a nuisance. On more than one occasion, the townspeople had to call the sheriff's office to complain about a naked man riding a horse down Main Street. That man was Victor Tillmans, and he was showing classic signs of dementia.

At 70, Victor had good days and bad days, but mostly going half-mad days. While his face was full of wrinkles, his rugged "Marlboro Man" looks made him popular with the female residents of Shady Acres. His adult children had admitted him there against his will and he had attempted to escape on multiple occasions. Unfortunately for Victor, it wasn't too hard for the authorities to find him once he went missing; all they had to do was wait for reports of a naked man walking down the street.

Today was a Monday and that meant Victor would be receiving his weekly cookie from his former co-star Elizabeth Pierce. Ever since the last season of *Casa Grande*, Elizabeth would bake cookies and send one to Victor each Monday, then follow up with a phone call, always at three p.m., where she would say nothing but "I hope you enjoy my cookie, Victor." He thought this was sweet, especially given that he had broken off their off-screen affair more than two decades earlier. He knew Elizabeth was a vindictive woman, which is why he thought it strange that she would do anything kind for him.

Just as he began to pull the shades down, there was a knock at the door, followed by the arrival of Arlene, Victor's favorite nurse. "Mr. Tillmans," Arlene said. "Your Monday package came. Do you want me to leave it on your dresser?"

"Why must you insist on asking me the same question every single week?" Victor said angrily. "Yes, please leave it on my dresser like you always do."

"What's bothering you today, Mr. Tillmans? Not having a good day?"

Victor began to soften; it was hard to stay mad at someone as sweet as Arlene. "I'm sorry, dear, but no, I'm not having a good day...no, make that a good month... no, make that a good year! My family sent me to this place and they never visit. On top of that it's been years since I've had a roll in the hay. Say, Arlene, what you do say you close that door and come a little closer?"

"That's the Victor I know! Always trying to get a little sumpin' sumpin'. You know I can't do that, Mr. Tillmans, but I can help you open that box."

"Well, you can't blame a dirty old man for trying, can you...?" Victor stared at her blindly, realizing that he could not remember her name.

"Arlene. It's me, Arlene, Mr. Tillmans."

"Of course, Arlene. Yes, please help me open that box."

After Arlene opened the box and gave him the cookie, she left to check on her other patients. Victor turned his attention to his notebook. He had learned that it was best to write down his thoughts when he had moments of clarity. His latest entry involved notes about how he would break out of Shady Acres without getting caught. He recognized his own handwriting immediately and read:

Victor, ask yourself what goes wrong with every escape attempt. Here's a hint: for some reason you (we) always do it naked. The next time you (we) escape, that is exactly what they will be looking for. So think, old man—how can you (we) escape and get away with it? The answer is simple: don't just wear clothes; wear a disguise! Dress up like a woman and you (we) are more likely to get away with it. Halloween is coming up—tell that sweet piece of tail, Arlene, that you (we) would like to order a costume for Halloween and see if she will help you. Explain that Marilyn Monroe is your (our) favorite actress and then have her help you (us) source a Marilyn costume. Let's call this operation Victor Victoria and get out of this loony bin as soon as you (we) can!

After reading his letter to himself, Victor hit the nurse button located at his bedside table. Arlene appeared within seconds.

"I was wondering—could you help me order a

39

Halloween costume?"

"That's the spirit, Mr. Tillmans. I'd be happy to. What did you have in mind?"

Victor walked over to his dresser to find his wallet. He gave her two hundred-dollar bills. "Make me look like Marilyn Monroe and you can keep the change."

"Not a problem, Mr. Tillmans. I'm happy to help." With that, Arlene left the room to take care of Victor's next-door neighbor, who had just begun singing loudly like Ethel Merman.

"I've got to get out of here," Victor mumbled softly to himself. He looked at his watch; it was three p.m. Like clockwork, his phone began to ring; he picked it up, said hello, and listened to the gravelly voice on the other end of the line state simply, "I hope you enjoy my cookie, Victor," and then hang up.

CHAPTER NINE
Acting Class

Blaze Hazelwood entered a focus group at an office building in Calabasas, with five other teachers from the Los Virgenes Unified School District. But today he wasn't Blaze Hazelwood: He was posing as Brian Bourcier, a ninth-grade Language Arts teacher from Westlake Village. When it was his turn, Blaze introduced himself to the group and sized up his fellow teachers. He took a particular interest in Natalie, a seventh-grade English teacher. *Oh, goodie,* Blaze thought to himself. In his experience, English teachers often had a hidden wild side.

After *Casa Grande*, Blaze had gone on to tackle the lead role in a musical production of *Back to the Future*, and, as Marty McFly, had the opportunity to show off not only his acting but his singing and dancing as well.

On opening night, the theater was sold out. Thousands of adult women flocked to the Christopher Lloyd Theatre on 43rd Street to see their heartthrob Blaze Hazelwood take to the stage, only to be sorely disappointed—the show opened to scathing reviews, with one reviewer writing,

"This show smells worse than the pile of manure Biff winds up in during Act One." After the first night, attendance died down, until by the end of the week the producers couldn't even give the tickets away.

Remarkably for Blaze, even this fiasco didn't end his career. The press went easy on him, blaming poor writing, subpar musical direction, and bad choreography instead of the show's star. The only silver lining to come out of the show was a Tony Award nomination for songwriter James Morgan's "I'm Your Density." Sung by actor Tony Scott, who played the part of George McFly, a studio version of the song received widespread airplay across radio stations in the US for the entire summer of 1989. The house party club remix of the song had even experienced a resurgence in recent years, along with everything '80s.

Blaze was still offered parts after that, but his confidence was shaken. After filming a pilot for a major network, he was offered the chance to attend a focus group organized by the network to gauge viewer reaction. Blaze had never been to a focus group before and was hesitant to attend, as he felt that regular people shouldn't be deciding whether or not a show gets the green light. However, the network twisted his arm, so he relented and went to observe the session.

That first group was held at an office building in Westwood, California – not far from UCLA. From behind a one-way mirror, Blaze watched six people enter a room and introduce themselves to the interviewer. There was Becky, a homemaker from Brentwood, and Phillip, an electrician from Torrance. There was also Tori, a teacher, and Kathy, a lawyer, both from Hermosa Beach.

Rounding out the group were Charlie, an accountant from Santa Monica, and Hillary, a drag queen from West Hollywood. What this mismatched group of people could say about the pilot, Blaze didn't know. As he watched the group, Blaze saw each participant as a character, making him wonder whether focus groups might be a way of building his acting chops and gaining more confidence.

Leaving the group, which fortunately for Blaze was rather positive toward the pilot, he asked the receptionist, Mary, "So do you only test TV shows here, or do you test other things?"

"Oh, heavens, no," Mary replied. "Last night we tested different types of toothpaste and tomorrow we are testing packaging options for a lawn fertilizer."

"Fascinating," Blaze replied. "Tell me, what does one have to do to be invited to these sessions?"

"Well, we have a list of people who have agreed to participate in research and we go down the list. The people who qualify get invited. It's easy peasy."

"Easy peasy indeed, luv," Blaze said while turning on his British affectation. "Tell me, how can I get my name on your special list?"

"Oh, Mr. Hazelwood, why would a star like you want to participate in some boring research sessions?"

Blaze explained that he wanted to practice playing different characters. Mary initially objected, fearing that it would compromise the research process, but surrendered when Blaze's piercing blue eyes looked deeply into her eyes. With his hands placed on top of hers he said, "Please." It was all too much for Mary to handle and she acquiesced. Fifteen years later, Blaze had participated in hundreds of focus groups, dressed in various disguises, and his acting had become stronger and stronger, although if critics were privy to these focus group performances they might have suggested he was better in the focus groups than he was on screen.

At the conclusion of this evening's group, which happened to be about electronic textbooks, Blaze followed Natalie out to her car. "Excuse me, Natalie, is it?" Blaze said, knowing full well what her name was. "I thought what you had to say about digital textbooks was brilliant."

"I can't believe the other people in the group didn't feel the same way," Natalie replied. "You were the only one to come to my aid—thank you, Brian."

"My pleasure. Hey, this money is burning a hole in my pocket," Blaze said, referring to the $150 cash incentive each group member received for his or her participation. "What do you say I treat you to dinner? I know a great place not too far from here, the best Italian food you'll find west of Arthur Avenue." Blaze referenced the street in The Bronx known for its authentic Italian food and the occasional mob hit.

Natalie was caught off guard, but she recovered quickly. "I don't see why not. Do you mind driving? I'm a little low on fuel."

"No problem." Blaze walked her over to his car, a new convertible Porsche Boxster.

"This is a pretty nice set of wheels for a teacher," Natalie said.

"I wasn't always a teacher, luv" Blaze said with a mischievous wink, and with that they were off.

CHAPTER TEN

The Ice Queen

Four weeks after the launch of *Bling It On Featuring T-Bang*, Allison Hart found herself in Brandon Master's office, unsure whether the meeting had been called to cheer her or jeer her. On the positive side, with five million people, mostly 15-to-18-year-old boys, streaming *Bling It On* every week, Allison knew she had a hit on her hands; sales of UPC's Lust line of products had gone through the roof. However, she was nervous that some of the antics recorded by T-Bang and his crew might be too much for UPC to handle. For example, the show was extremely profane—it seemed T-Bang and his crew couldn't go more than two minutes without using a curse word or making a joke involving one bodily function or another. While they weren't held to the same standards as network television, Allison was nervous that the show was crossing a line.

Brandon broke the silence first. "Allison, I wanted to tell you how much we love what you have been doing for the Lust brand. I just got off the phone with the brand team and they say that their biggest challenge is keeping up customer inventory. I believe this is a direct result of your show on Pocket Box."

Allison's heart started to beat at a more normal pace. "It's really a team effort, sir."

"If there is one thing you need to learn, Allison," Brandon said, "it's to not be so humble. Humble people never rise up the ladder in this business. You put this concept together, you signed the talent, and you should get the credit."

Just then, Brandon's phone buzzed. "What is it, Margo?" Margo had been Brandon's personal assistant for close to 20 years. She'd had four plastic surgeries, including a face-lift, a boob job, a nose job, and liposuction. At 57, she dressed more like a teenager than a grandmother, which she had become earlier that year.

"Catherine Philips is here to see you, Brandon. Shall I send her in?"

Catherine Philips was the general manager of UPC's Believe brand, which included a full range of products, including hair care, face care, body wash, moisturizer, and deodorant. Believe was the biggest skincare brand in the world, surpassing one billion dollars in sales each year in the United States alone. The sum of all of UPC's other personal care brands together wouldn't come close to Believe's annual sales.

The announcement of Catherine's arrival puzzled Allison. While Brandon's calendar was always booked back to back, she never knew him to double-book meetings. Knowing how important Catherine was, Allison started to say "If you need me to come back—" but Brandon did not let her finish the sentence.

"No, stay right there. Catherine is the reason why I

called this meeting. Send her in please, Margo."

Catherine walked into the room as if she owned it. Wearing a charcoal Balmain suit that cost as much as Allison's first car, a pair of Louboutin shoes that cost more than Allison's suit, and carrying an Yves St. Laurent bag that easily exceeded what Allison paid in monthly rent for her Manhattan Beach apartment, Catherine was the epitome of the modern-day successful corporate woman. Allison, who had never experienced a lack of confidence before, felt intimidation spread from the bottom of her feet all the way to the top of her head.

"Brandon, darling, sorry I am so late," Catherine said, kissing Brandon on both cheeks. "I got caught up in a brand review meeting that was put on by the market research department. At some point I'd like to know what planet we hire those people from." Catherine's disdain for anything that smelled of consumer research was well known throughout the company. She believed it was the job of the marketer to tell consumers what they want, not the consumer's job to voice their opinions to the brand.

"No worries at all, Catherine," Brandon said, holding her gaze a second longer than he should have. With a movement of his hand in Allison's general direction, he said, "I'd like to introduce you to Allison Hart."

"Congratulations on the success of your show. Those boys on the Lust team can't stop talking about it."

All Allison could manage was, "Thank you." Allison was used to being the tallest woman in a room, but Catherine had her beat by at least two inches. Further, it appeared that Catherine was made of pure muscle; there was not an ounce of fat that Allison could detect on her body. To top it off, Catherine's brunette bob suggested she was strictly business; and this was confirmed with the tone she used when addressing most subordinates. A former assistant characterized Catherine as having the looks of a young Barbara Hershey with the personality of an angry Martha Stewart.

"And that is why I wanted to have this meeting," Brandon said. "As I mentioned on the phone, Catherine, I really think Allison here can help you with the launch of Project Fountain."

Project Fountain was the code name for a new product line to be launched under the Believe brand. "Fountain" was short for Fountain of Youth; the Believe team had developed a product that visibly reduced the signs of aging, so long as the user followed a certain product regimen. The product line would be launched with both men's and women's varieties, and the company was spending more than $200 million on the launch—more money than had ever been spent to launch a personal care product in history.

"I'm flattered that you think I can help," Allison said, "but I'm not sure what I can do. The Pocket Box platform is really geared to young adults 18–24. I'm not sure that the core Believe user even knows what Pocket Box is."

Catherine looked Allison directly in the eyes, and Allison felt a chill run through her body. "Allison, I have no intention of having my brand promoted through some online reality show. We have another opportunity that I'd like to discuss."

Brandon interjected, "What if we could take your reality model and adapt it to a more 'silver' audience?"

Catherine interrupted, "This line is being targeted to men and women 50 years of age and older. This age range not only represents the fastest-growing consumer segment, but they also have the most disposable income. Additionally, they all want to look younger. We know we have a hit on our hands and we want to maximize product exposure; that's where you come in."

"If a network audience is what you're looking for," Allison said, "why not just advertise on network TV?"

"Because even though this segment isn't as tech-savvy, they are still shifting their viewing and skipping commercials," Catherine countered. "We need you to create something they can relate to and make the product a hero of that show."

Brandon said, "UPC owns the Universal Broadcasting Network, so I can influence the head of programming to greenlight any idea you come up with, as long as it's good. Given your track record with *Bling It On*, half the work is already done. If you nail Fountain, too, you can write your own ticket inside UPC."

"Talk to your team and come back to us in two weeks with ideas," Catherine said.

"I'll have Margo reach out to get some time on the calendar," Brandon said. "That's all. I have another matter to discuss with Catherine." That was Allison's cue to leave.

There had been rumors going around about an affair between Brandon and Catherine, but Allison had thought they were just that, rumors. After all, Catherine was married to Brian Philips, the chairman and chief executive officer of UPC. The much publicized Rosdale–Philips wedding had been the social event of the previous summer. But now Allison wasn't so sure.

On the walk back to her office, fuming with resentment

at being talked down to, Allison had a thought: If she could somehow find evidence of an affair between Brandon and Catherine, she could use this information to climb higher in the organization. Her mood began to brighten.

Upon reaching her office, she had Marios call her assistant producer Lucy Nichols, as well as Bruce Biller, a UPC exec who formerly led one of the world's leading advertising agencies. The three were the team who conceived of the idea for *Bling It On Featuring T-Bang*, and Allison wanted to tap into their collective brain power to craft a show for Project Fountain. When they arrived, Allison wasted no time getting down to business.

"First off," Allison said, "what are the latest numbers for *Bling It On?*"

Lucy replied, "The audience grows every week. Last night's streaming almost broke Twitter." Allison thought that Lucy almost seemed giddy; but then again, Lucy's curly red hair and freckled complexion always made her appear giddy.

"What do you mean?" Allison asked.

Bruce, with his trademark five o'clock shadow and shoulder-length hair, spoke up, "Well, T-Bang and the boys were making last-minute changes to the plans for his 25th birthday party, which is all set for tomorrow night. Last night this meant going to West Hollywood and auditioning drag queens. They had them do everything from impressions, to strip teases, and even stand-up comedy. They handed out invitations to those who they considered to be worthy enough to join them at the party, which they were referring to as the party to end all parties. Apparently, the volume of tweets from the audience was so high, Twitter almost crashed. That people were so interested in seeing what tricks T-Bang had up his sleeve was reassuring to Allison, who needed to keep interest in *Bling it On* as high as possible.

Allison shook her head. "I really can't believe we are getting away with this. Lucy, did you confirm with the Lust team that all the product had been shipped to T-Bang's parents' house in Malibu?" The Lust brand had agreed to cover any and all non-alcohol related expenses for the party, provided T-Bang provide samples of Lust to all of his guests.

"They've been shipped and received," Lucy said.

"Great, one more thing to check off the list. Now, there's something else that we need to talk about." Allison relayed the details of the meeting with Brandon and Catherine.

"So they basically want to replicate *Bling It On*, but featuring someone that my parents would find interesting? How the hell are we going to pull that off?"

Little did they know, the answer to their question was closer to T-Bang than they could possibly imagine.

CHAPTER ELEVEN

Have You Seen Molly?

You've still got it, Blazey boy, Blaze Hazelwood thought to himself as he escorted Natalie into a restaurant that no teacher could afford. They were shown to their table and ordered cocktails, a Grey Goose and soda for Blaze and a Cosmopolitan for Natalie.

Just as Natalie was about to question who he really was, a waiter came over and, even though Blaze was dressed in a disguise, recognized him immediately. "Oh, Mr. Hazelwood, so good to see you. Were you shooting today? You look different, it must be the makeup."

Upon hearing his surname, a light bulb went off in Natalie's head. "Oh, my God, you're Blaze Hazelwood, from that show...the one about the winemaking family."

With that, he removed the wig and glasses he was wearing and said, "Guilty as charged."

"But why are you doing focus groups, do you need the money or something?"

"Heavens no, luv, I do the groups to understand regular people, so I can play them better on TV and in movies."

"How long have you been doing this for?" Natalie asked.

"Long enough," Blaze replied, while running his foot up her leg. He had removed his shoes upon sitting down at the table. As his foot ran up and down her leg, Natalie started to blush.

Their cocktails came and they ordered dinner. Blaze was careful not to talk about himself too much. Naturally Natalie was interested in his celebrity, and Blaze obliged her with insights into his professional life, but he was mindful to also ask her questions about herself. Someone had once told him that any man could have a woman eating out of his hands if he simply showed an interest in her. The questions seemed to be working like a charm, so Blaze said, "What do you say we skip dessert and go someplace quieter where we can talk? I don't live too far from here."

Natalie nodded her agreement.

Blaze took her to his place in Malibu, not far from the restaurant. When they arrived, his neighbors were having what appeared to be a pretty wild party; Blaze was surprised, since the woman was a retired actress and her husband was a lawyer and as exciting as a head of lettuce. When he got out of the car and heard the club music he realized that it wasn't the parents who were hosting the party but their son, Thaddeus, who Blaze remembered went by the name T-Rex, or T-Bird, or something like that. After pulling into his driveway he noticed a woman crawling on all fours on the patch of grass that separated the two homes. She was wearing a bright red sequined dress and four-inch-high heels to match.

"Can I help you?" Blaze asked.

Not bothering to look up from where she was crawling, the woman replied, in an unusually deep voice, "Have you seen Molly?"

"And who might Molly be?" Blaze inquired.

"Molly is not a who, it's a what," the woman replied.

Puzzled, Blaze just shook his head. He had more pressing matters to attend to, such as getting Natalie into something more comfortable.

"Aren't you going to help that woman?" Natalie asked.

"I'm not a babysitter," Blaze replied. "I'm sure one of her friends will come get her. Now, how about you and I have a nightcap inside?"

The two walked through Blaze's front door and were greeted by a life-size cutout of Blaze himself adorning his foyer. Natalie appeared startled by this. She examined this other Blaze more closely and noticed that it had some writing on it. "What language is that?"

"German, my dear. It was a gift from a fan. David Hasselhoff and I have a little wager going, to see who can receive the most outlandish gifts from their German fans."

"I don't think you are going to win with a cardboard cutout of yourself," Natalie said, not hiding her sarcasm.

"Look a bit more closely, luv." Blaze pointed down at the cardboard Blaze's pelvis area; where his penis should have been, there was nothing but a hole.

"I don't understand," Natalie said, confused.

"A fan of mine had this made. She had her husband stand behind it while she gave him oral sex so she could pretend that she was servicing me. Then she mailed it to me as a gift, along with a few pictures of them in action. Let's go have a seat on the couch and have a drink, what would you like?"

"Tequila over ice and a wedge of lime?"

Blaze's belief that English teachers had a wild side was confirmed by Natalie's choice of drink. Earlier that day Blaze heard a song called "Tequila Makes Her Clothes Fall Off" by Joe Nichols and was now convinced the song was prophetic.

Blaze left the room and Natalie made herself comfortable on his couch, looking through the window at the Pacific Ocean. Natalie heard a loud sound behind her and she turned her head to see what was happening in the neighbors' yard.

What she saw startled her. It was a group of young men holding lighters up to some kind of aerosol spray and making fireballs. Each fireball was followed with a slew of curse words and slang, which she typically only heard in movies starring Samuel L. Jackson.

"I am sorry for the sideshow going on next door," Blaze said, carrying their beverages in from the other room. "I had no idea that there would be a party over there tonight."

"I'm just amazed at how this new generation of kids behaves. In my day we just got stoned and listened to music. These kids seem to need a little bit more to get their rocks off." Natalie paused to take a sip of her drink. "Oh God, how I love the warmth tequila brings."

Blaze had learned the art of making a cocktail from his former co-star Victor Tillmans, the mustached actor who played Blaze's on-screen father, Barton Dixon, on *Casa Grande*. Victor had given him some sage advice when Blaze came of age.

"My mother used to say that the key to a man's heart is his

stomach. Bullshit. The key to a man's heart is his penis. Blaze, do you know how to get a woman to pay attention to your penis?"

"How, Victor?"

"By making her a good drink."

Blaze and his co-star Danny Maieye had spent most of their free time with Victor as he showed them how to make what he referred to as "ice-breakers." Victor also gave his protégés a stern warning.

"With great power comes great responsibility, gentlemen. You are both good-looking boys, and your faces are well-known. If a woman ever says no, respect that. Don't try to convince her to sleep with you just because you've got a hard-on for her."

Natalie asked a question that brought Blaze's attention back to the present day. "Don't you worry about your neighbors being able to see in your window?"

"It's a special kind of glass," Blaze replied. "We can see out, but they can't see in. From the outside, it looks like a mirror." Blaze had been inspired by all the focus groups he attended, with their one-way mirrors.

"You mean they can't see anything at all in here?" Natalie asked.

"Nothing, luv," Blaze responded.

At that moment, Natalie stood up in front of Blaze, looked him directly in the eye, and unbuttoned the two buttons on the front of her sundress. Blaze reached out to help her, but she said sternly, "Keep your hands to yourself...for now."

Natalie proceeded to untie the belt around her dress and, moments later, Blaze saw it fall to the floor. She had nothing on underneath and proceeded to show Blaze just how naughty a middle-school English teacher could be.

Blaze had been a devotee of the art of tantra ever since

befriending Sting in the mid-'80s. Their lovemaking session went on for what seemed like hours. Too exhausted to speak afterward, all they could do was breathe deeply.

A sudden noise outside shattered the silence that enveloped the living room after their respective climaxes. Looking out the window, Blaze noticed something odd in the bushes that divided his property from the neighbors. "Oh, bloody hell," Blaze said dialing up his British affectation even higher.

"What is it?" Natalie asked.

Blaze pointed toward the window. The deep-voiced woman in the red sequined dress and the high heels was facing the window of Blaze's house. Her dress was pulled up to her waist and she was peeing standing up. "Looks like the she is a he," Natalie remarked.

"That explains the voice," Blaze replied, and with that they collapsed on the couch, laughing.

CHAPTER TWELVE

A Man with One Red Shoe

The night was dragging on back at the Pocket Box offices, and Lucy Nichols was going blind watching the livestream of *Bling It On*. She was hoping for something sensational to happen at T-Bang's party, but so far the most exciting thing that she saw was one of T-Bang's friends accidentally light himself on fire after making what they called "Lust balls," which involved taking an open flame to a can of Lust and lighting the mist on fire. She wasn't sure that the Lust brand manager would be pleased about seeing the product used in this way, but then again, any publicity was good publicity, right?

Allison stopped by on her way out the door, annoyed about the meeting she'd had earlier with Brandon and Catherine, who she was now referring to as "the Ice Queen." She still had no idea how she was going to create magic for Project Fountain. "How's the party going?"

"J-Dog set himself on fire, but other than that everything is fine."

"Holy shit, is he okay?"

"Yeah," Lucy replied. "They were right next to the pool and T-Bang threw him in. Unfortunately, that's the most exciting thing that's happened all night."

"It's past midnight, what do you say we call it a day?"

Just as Lucy was going to take her boss up on the offer, she noticed a commotion on the screen. "Now what is this all about?" Lucy asked.

"It looks as if there is an irate gentleman approaching T-Bang. What is he carrying?"

"It looks like a red high-heeled shoe."

Once he was closer to T-Bang, Allison got a better look at him and asked Lucy, "Does he look familiar to you at all?"

"No, but look, he's packing some serious heat." Lucy was referring to the bulge in his pants.

"You aren't kidding! I wonder what this is all about." *Maybe this day can be saved after all*, Allison thought.

#

Blaze and Natalie had dozed off on his couch and were awoken by the sound of shattering glass.

"What the hell was that?" Blaze asked. "Are you okay?"

"I'm fine," Natalie replied. "But I think that party is getting out of hand."

Blaze looked around and found a red high-heeled shoe in the middle of his family room where glass was shattered like feathers after a pillow fight. Furious, he picked the glass out of his pants and put them on, skipping the underwear and not bothering with a shirt.

"Where are you going?" Natalie asked.

"To deal with a T-Rex," Blaze replied.

On his way out the door he was confronted by what he

now knew was a man in drag wearing a red sequined dress and only one high-heeled shoe. "Have you seen Molly?" the man asked.

"If I find Molly," Blaze replied. "I am going to shove her up your ass."

With that, he stomped through his neighbor's yard to find the host of the party.

#

T-Bang had just finished taking a swig of Cristal when he noticed a shirtless man coming toward him holding a red high-heeled shoe in his hand. One of his friends remarked to him, "Which one of these things is not like the other, bro?"

"I'm looking for T-Rex, or T-Bird, or whoever the hell it is responsible for this party."

"Yo, my name is T-Bang, G, why you trippin'?"

"I'm trippin' because this party is becoming a T-pain in my ass. One of your guests just threw her, or should I say his, shoe through my window."

"Is that the bitch who was looking for Molly, yo, J-Dog, I told you we shouldn't have invited those 'vesties." Turning his attention back to Blaze, T-Bang said, "Let's take a walk."

It was 12:30 in the morning, and Blaze looked around and saw what appeared to be 50 or so young women wearing nothing but bikinis and many others who were topless. The property was completely trashed, but this didn't seem to bother T-Bang at all.

"Look, I'm sorry about your window," T-Bang said. Gone was his ghetto speak. "It's my 25th birthday and things are getting out of hand. I'll cover the cost to replace your window and I'll try to keep it down. We cool?"

Blaze was taken aback by T-Bang's civility and wondered if he was just another wild child trying to be someone he wasn't. "Yes, we're cool," Blaze replied. "Just no more projectiles coming through my window if you please."

"Deal. I'll walk you out." T-Bang escorted Blaze around the corner and back toward his house when they both noticed someone passed out in a lounge chair, one foot hanging over the edge, a red heel on the ground below it. Blaze walked over, knelt down by the chair, and put the shoe back on its owner's foot.

T-Bang exclaimed, "You're a real Prince Charming, aren't you?"

"I've been called worse." And with that, Blaze headed back home.

#

"Well, that was interesting," Lucy said. "I was kind of hoping there was going to be a fistfight. We need some good TV."

Allison didn't hear a word Lucy said. "I'm pretty sure that was Blaze Hazelwood."

"Blaze Hazel who?" Lucy asked.

"Hazelwood," Allison replied. "My grandmother and I would watch his show, *Casa Grande*, whenever I would sleep over at her house. He was a real heartthrob back in the day.

"*Casa Grande* was one of the biggest shows of the '80s. The final episode was one of the most-watched TV episodes of all time, right behind the final episode of *M*A*S*H*. I'm guessing he's, what, 43 or 44 now?"

"Let me check IMDB." Lucy pulled up the website on

her computer. "He's 45. Looks like he went from A-list to B-list since his *Casa Grande* days. He seems to be just doing a lot of voice work now."

"He might be just what we need for Project Fountain! Lucy, when I come in tomorrow morning I want to know where all the stars on *Casa Grande* wound up. I'm going to find out whether the mansion where they filmed the show is still standing—I have an idea of how we can use it."

"What happened to my being able to go home?"

"Plans change. No time for sleep. This could be the break we need."

CHAPTER THIRTEEN

Sins in the Confessional

Father Daniel Maieye was dreading the meeting he was about to have with his superior, Monsignor Paul Allen, who was rumored to be friends with the bishop himself. It was the eve of Daniel's tenth anniversary of entering religious life and he knew that he was in hot water over an event that had occurred a few days before.

"Father Daniel," Monsignor Allen started off, "I had great reservations about you from the moment you were ordained. I questioned whether a former actor would be the right priest for our diocese. I was happy to have been proven wrong in that regard."

It was true that Father Daniel had an energy about him that other priests in the diocese didn't: he was young, attractive, and able to lean on a wealth of world experience when giving a homily. His masses were the most highly attended masses at his parish. He truly seemed to have turned his life around and found his true calling.

"Thank you for the kind words, Monsignor," Danny

said.

Monsignor Allen continued, "It has come to my attention, though, Father Daniel, that you may have recently broken one of your priestly vows." .

Daniel knew exactly where this was going. For the past ten years as an ordained priest, and the previous five years while in seminary, Danny had led a celibate life, following the tradition in the Catholic Church for priests and nuns. This was very challenging for a guy who was rumored to have bedded over 2,000 women during his time on *Casa Grande* and, later, as the leader of the rock band Sinner's Swing. But he remained faithful to his vows.

Over the past few weeks, Father Daniel had noticed the choir director, Kathleen Guilard, starting to flirt with him. It started off innocently enough: She began to hold eye contact with him for a second longer than usual. Then came the subtle touching; she would grab his wrist or place her hand on his elbow. Recently, however, she had become more forward, texting him throughout the day and even sending him pictures of her in various states of undress. While "Danny Boy" would have taken advantage of the situation, "Father Daniel" wanted nothing to do with it; it was hard enough staying faithful to one's vow of celibacy when women weren't flirting with him, but it was damn near impossible to do so when they were.

Five days earlier, Father Daniel had found himself in the confessional before the five p.m. mass on Saturday. Typically he was lucky if two or three people came to confess their sins, so he was surprised when, after his third penitent had left the confessional, a fourth came in.

In the confessional, the penitent has the choice to confess their sins through a screen, for anonymity, or face to face, and the fourth penitent that Saturday afternoon chose the latter. Father Daniel recognized Kathleen immediately and began to feel uncomfortable.

Kathleen started off by crossing herself and proclaiming, "Bless me, Father, for I am about to sin..."

Father Daniel interrupted, "About to sin?" but before he could say another word Kathleen pulled her dress over her head and lunged at him.

The penitent who had been in the confessional previously was still in a pew, praying the penance that Father Daniel suggested, when she heard a commotion coming from inside the confessional. She opened the door and saw Kathleen Guilard, now in nothing but her undergarments, sitting astride Father Daniel. Daniel shouted, "It's not what you think!" but the penitent ran screaming from the church.

Monsignor Allen, who was away on vacation at the time, came back to a stack of mail that included a strongly written letter from the penitent who had walked in on Father Daniel and the choir director.

"I knew you were too good to be true, Daniel," Monsignor Allen proclaimed. "I suppose we were all foolish to believe that a former bad boy of Hollywood could become a man of the cloth."

"Monsignor," Daniel pleaded, "it's not what it seems. She came on to me, I was trying to push her off of me."

"Do you expect me to believe that!" The monsignor's words echoed throughout the entire rectory. "What makes more sense, a former Hollywood star turned priest takes a withdrawal out of his bank of bad habits, or a faithful choir director who has served this parish for the better part of 10 years finds you so irresistible that she disrobes in a confessional and holds you against your will? She has a 10-year-old son who is an altar boy here, for goodness sake!"

Daniel tried to retort, "Look, I know it's hard to believe," but he couldn't finish his sentence before the monsignor interrupted.

"It was easier for Doubting Thomas to believe that Christ was risen from the dead than it is for me to believe that you didn't have a role in this. I've made up my mind. I am placing you on administrative leave while we investigate this matter in more detail. If I so much as uncover that you kissed another parishioner on the cheek, I will have you defrocked. During this period, you will not be able to celebrate the mass, and you will not be able to live at the rectory."

"Where am I supposed to live then?" Daniel argued. "I gave all of my savings to the church; I can't afford to live anywhere else."

"That's not my problem," the monsignor replied. "You must be out of the rectory by five p.m. tonight."

With that, the meeting was clearly over, and Father Daniel found himself numb from head to toe. He didn't have any family in the area, and most of the people from his former life wanted nothing to do with him. There was one person he could count on, though, one person he had been intending to visit for a very long time. Victor Tillmans. He had heard that Victor was now living in a retirement home in Westlake Village, just a few miles up the 101 freeway from where Danny was at the moment. *No time like the present*, he said to himself. Having made up his mind to see his old friend that evening, Father Daniel returned to the rectory, packed a bag of clothes and placed his few valuables into a box, got into his SUV, and started driving north.

CHAPTER FOURTEEN

Victor Makes a Break for It

The staff of the Shady Acres retirement home was busy putting up last-minute decorations for the residents' Halloween party when a voice over the intercom announced that nurse Arlene was needed on the third floor. She put down the paper bat she was holding, turned to her colleagues, and said, "I have five minutes before I'm off for the night. If that old man makes another pass at me, so help me God, I'm going to put something in his orange juice tomorrow morning."

Arlene arrived at Victor Tillmans' room and couldn't believe her eyes. "Mr. Tillmans, is that you? You shaved your trademark mustache."

"The one and only," he replied—except he wasn't a he, he was a she! Dressed in a long white dress with a blonde wig on his head and a pearl necklace around his neck, Victor Tillmans had transformed himself into the spitting image of Marilyn Monroe, albeit a wrinkly, 70-year-old Marilyn Monroe.

"I must say, Mr. Tillmans, I wouldn't have recognized

you if I weren't the one who purchased that costume for you. Is there something you needed?"

"Arlene, be a love and help me with my lipstick. I was never good at putting on makeup; we always had professionals who did it for us. If I did it myself, I fear I'd look like one of those bozos from the band KISS."

"No problem, Mr. Tillmans." While Arlene was resentful for having to do this right before the end of her shift, she did have a soft spot in her heart for Victor and felt as if he really didn't need to be in the home. While he had some off days with his memory, most of the time he was pretty sharp.

"Tell me, Arlene, will you be staying for the party tonight?"

"No, Mr. Tillmans," Arlene replied. "I promised my kids I would take them out trick-or-treating."

This news made Victor very happy. Arlene was the only one who knew Victor was going to the party dressed as Marilyn Monroe; if she wasn't there, his escape could be cleaner. "That's too bad, I was hoping to boogie to the *Monster Mash* with you out on the dance floor."

"I'll have to take a rain check on that, Mr. Tillmans." She put the lipstick down and touched up his cheeks with blush, then smiled at the fruits of her labor. "I think that just about does it, Mr. Tillmans. I hope you have a good time at the party."

"Stay safe trick-or-treating with your kids tonight, Arlene. There are a bunch of crazies out there."

#

Father Daniel entered the lobby of the Shady Acres nursing home at 7:30 p.m. He didn't bother changing out of his Roman collar and cassock and was greeted by the receptionist as if he were in costume.

"Let me guess," the receptionist said, "you're dressed up as Father What-a-waste; am I right? You look like a young Joe DiMaggio in a priest's outfit."

Father Daniel had heard that one before—it was a waste, she was saying, that such a good-looking man was living a celibate life. While he typically took it as a compliment, at that moment he was starting to think his good looks might be undermining his ministry; clearly they were responsible for his current predicament.

"I appreciate the compliment"—Father Daniel looked down at the woman's chest to see her name tag—"Sarah, but I am the real deal. I'm here to visit with Victor Tillmans."

"Oh, pardon me, Father, let me ring his room. Is he expecting you?"

"No, I kind of wanted to surprise him."

"I just love Victor, such a sweet man." Sarah called his room, but no one picked up. "Let me just look up something for a second." Sarah looked at the log book to see which of the residents had checked out and didn't see Victor's name on the list. "Well, he should be here; maybe he came down already for the party. Do you want to just go down the hall to our common room and see if you can find him? Usually we require visitors to be escorted either by their guests or a member of our staff, but I think we can make an exception in your case."

Father Daniel was walking toward the common room when he was knocked over by an elderly woman dressed as Marilyn Monroe. "I'm terribly sorry," Father Daniel said, but she stood up, turned her back to him, and walked toward the reception area.

When he reached the common room, he saw no sight of his old friend and co-star Victor Tillmans; he asked various staffers if they had seen him and they all said no. He then asked an orderly if he wouldn't mind escorting him to Victor's room, and upon arrival they both saw that the room was empty. "That's odd," the orderly said. "Mr. Tillmans is almost always in his room, and when he isn't he's usually in the common room. I wonder where he could be."

"Is there something I could help you with?" a voice at the door said. It was Ginny, the head nurse in charge of the night shift.

"The good father is here to see Mr. Tillmans," the orderly said. "But we can't seem to find him anywhere."

"I'm sure he will turn up somewhere; he always does. Charles," Ginny said, addressing the orderly, "will you please tell Security that Mr. Tillmans is missing again and to keep an eye out for him?"

"Again?" Father Daniel muttered. "Does he go missing often?"

"Victor has been trying to break out of this place since the day his family moved him in. I anticipate we'll get a call from the sheriff's office soon about one of our residents roaming the streets of Westlake Village in the nude. That will be our good old Victor; he once made it all the way to Agoura Hills before anyone found him."

"Did you say in the nude?" Father Daniel asked.

"Well, your friend Victor isn't as sharp as he used to be. For whatever reason, whenever he escapes the first thing he does is remove all his clothing. The good thing for us is that's how we find him quickly."

"I see," Father Daniel said, handing Ginny a business card. "Can you do me a favor and call me once you do find him? I really would like to speak with him."

"Of course, Father," Ginny said. "Who could refuse a request from a priest as handsome as you?"

With that, Father Daniel left Ginny and Charles in Victor's room and headed toward the elevator. If what Ginny said was true, he wanted to drive around the streets of Westlake Village in hopes of finding Victor before the sheriff's office did. He also had to figure out where he was going to stay for the night; he didn't want to spend what little money he had on a hotel room. He figured he could always sleep in his SUV if he needed to. A few years ago he had purchased a used Chevy Tahoe that he used to help deliver food donations to various food banks around the area. That truck, and a small duffle bag of clothes, was all he had to his name.

He got into the Tahoe, put on his seatbelt, started the ignition, and backed out of his parking space. After leaving the grounds of Shady Acres, he was scared half to death when a voice began singing, "Oh, Danny boy, the pipes, the pipes are calling…"

Father Daniel stepped on the brakes and the Tahoe came to a stop. He turned around and looked in the back of the SUV, where he saw an elderly man dressed in drag as Marilyn Monroe. "Victor, is that you?"

"Oh, it's me, Danny Boy. I had to dress up in order to get out. I saw you pull in from my window, so I made a beeline for your truck. Sorry to startle you, but when you arrived I thought my prayers had been answered. Speaking of which, why are you dressed like a priest— aren't you a little old for trick-or-treating?"

Daniel pulled the truck over to the side of the road and quickly filled Victor in on the events of his last 15 years, up until the meeting he'd had with the monsignor that afternoon. "Hey, it's not like you are a kid-toucher," Victor said. "They should be happy that you tried to canoodle with a woman; most of those guys canoodle with each other—no offense, Danny Boy."

"None taken," Daniel said. "But the truth is, I didn't make a pass at her, she attacked me! They are going to do an investigation, and until they reach a decision, I have no place to live."

"You know, Danny Boy," Victor said, "I may have a solution to your problem. I kept my place in Culver City. I've been trying to escape there ever since I was put in that old folks' home."

"Are you sure your wife didn't sell it?" Daniel asked.

"How could she sell what she doesn't know about?" Victor replied sharply. "You remember the good times—you, me, and…and…and…"

"Blaze," Daniel said.

"Yes, thank you, Blaze. Sometimes those memories are all that keep me going."

"That was a long time ago, Victor; I'm a different man now."

"Different, my ass," Victor said. "I've been on this earth for seven decades, and if there's one thing I've learned, it's that people don't change. Believe me, Danny Boy, this little episode may be the best thing that could have happened to you. You've still got your good looks, I bet you could find work as an actor if you tried."

Daniel shook off Victor's words, remembering from past experience that arguing with Victor was pointless.

"Listen, kid, we're going to have some fun now that we're both free men. Just take the 101 south to the 405 and get off on Culver."

When Daniel turned left to merge onto the 101, he realized Victor had gone a few minutes without saying anything. He glanced in the rearview mirror and found his passenger fast asleep, with his wig sliding down his face. *At least it will be a quiet ride*, he thought to himself. He considered calling the staff of the retirement home to let them know that Victor was fine and in his care, but considered that doing so may bring his reunion with Victor to a premature close. Instead, he turned on the radio, which was always set to the eighties channel on satellite radio; Father Daniel sang along to Tears for Fears while Victor snored away in the back seat.

CHAPTER FIFTEEN
A Plan is Hatched

The morning after T-Bang's 25th birthday party, Lucy had tracked down all of the stars of *Casa Grande*. "First off, Elizabeth Pierce has money problems and is facing eviction. Vanessa Crestwood is facing a fate even worse than that, obsolescence—she hasn't been hired for a paying acting job in at least five years."

"That explains it," Allison said.

"Explains what?" Lucy replied.

"Why I saw Vanessa on TVSN recently promoting a product; money must be tight."

"Really?" Lucy questioned. "What was the product?"

"Not important," Allison said, her cheeks flushing. "What about the rest of the cast?"

Lucy replied that she had called the nursing home where Victor Tillmans was living but had trouble reaching him. "He never seems to be in his room when I call and he never returns my messages."

"What about the others—who was the rock 'n' roll kid, Danny something or other?"

"Boy," Lucy replied. "Get this, he actually became a priest and goes by his birth name—Danny Maieye. I called the parish where he works and was told he was on an administrative leave, but they wouldn't give me any more details. I'm trying to track down someone in his family but am hitting a wall."

"Keep at it with those two," Allison said. "Tell me, what is Blaze Hazelwood up to these days?"

"That one is a bit tricky," Lucy admitted. "Blaze actually managed to have something of a career after *Casa Grande*. For whatever reason, he is huge in Germany, so he goes there at least twice a year for fan events that he is paid a handsome fee to attend."

"Okay, but what has he been working on? We have to find some angle to play so that he can't help but say yes to our idea."

"He's made his living recently doing voiceovers for cartoons and video games, as well as playing the male leads in Hallmark Hall of Fame movies; you know, the ones that are on around Christmastime? Ever since Peter Falk died, Blaze started getting hired for them. I get sucked into those so easily," Lucy confessed. "There was one on last Christmas where a woman's long-lost brother, played by Blaze, appears to be none other than Santa Claus himself—"

Allison cut her off. "Don't you have any dirt on him? Disgruntled ex-wife? Rumors about him and Asian boys? Financial problems?"

"Nothing of the sort. The only thing that could be an opportunity for us is his relationship with his not-so-super-agent Stanley."

"Don't tell me he's represented by Stanley; that guy is a

nightmare!" Allison was right. Whenever a producer heard the name Stanley, they knew it would lead to some form of trouble. His reputation was so infamous that he didn't even need a last name, which he had of course. Roth, though that wasn't the name he was born with—his real name was Reilly McMurphy; when asked why he changed his name to Stanley Roth, Reilly, that is Stanley, would always reply, "Professional reasons."

Even more infamous than the story behind his name was the toupee he wore to cover up the fact that he was balder than a cue ball. This earned him the nickname "Stanley the Rug" within Hollywood circles.

"What do you want me to do?" Lucy asked.

"Have Marios set up a lunch between me and Stanley for this afternoon. He'll likely refuse because he won't recognize my name."

"How could he not know who you are? You are practically leading a revolution in the world of television!"

"Because he's a dinosaur," Allison said. "I can guarantee he doesn't have a smartphone; he probably still accesses the Internet from AOL dial-up. He'll have no idea that the hottest thing on the small screen these days is being streamed over the Internet and not broadcast to TV."

"So how will Marios get him to take a meeting with you if he doesn't know who you are?"

"Easy. Have Marios explain that lunch is on me and we have an opportunity that his client Blaze simply won't want to pass up, one that will make them both millions. He won't be able to resist."

CHAPTER SIXTEEN

Lunch with Stanley

Stanley was sitting in front of his computer waiting for it to connect to AOL when his phone rang and dropped the signal. "It never fails," he said to Boomer, his cat. "Whenever I want to go online someone always calls." At forty pounds overweight and with thinning hair covered by a bad toupee, Stanley looked like a cross between veteran character actor Dennis Franz and Hal Linden; both of whom played mustached detectives on TV. He would make a perfect supporting cast member on a cop show himself, if he had any talent.

Stanley picked up the phone and with a disdainful tone said, "Roth," using only his little-known last name. He listened to the voice on the other end and then replied, "Allison who? Hart—oh, never heard of her. No thanks, I have lunch plans."

The voice on the other end of the phone was persistent, though, and must have said something convincing because Stanley's demeanor changed immediately. "Oh, you don't say. Yes, okay, Delmonico's. No, it's no problem, I can move my lunch plans around. Okay, tell her I will see here there at 12:30. You too. Thanks, goodbye."

The fact of the matter was, Stanley hadn't had a business lunch in more than six months. Blaze Hazelwood was his only working client, and Blaze had threatened to fire him unless bigger roles started coming his way. Stanley was hopeful that this might be just the break he needed in order to remain a player in the business.

Allison waited at a two-top table in a private corner of Delmonico's restaurant. The restaurant was a mainstay of the Hollywood elite; on any given day you could see a virtual who's who of actors, directors, producers, and writers dining there. Allison looked at the clock on her phone and noted that Stanley was now 15 minutes late for their lunch. She hated when people were late.

Allison's mentors had taught her that a proper business lunch should be exactly 90 minutes long and follow a certain arc: small talk and compliments before lunch was ordered, discussing the business at hand while waiting for the food to be served, ironing out the details over the main course, and a celebration of whatever agreement was made over coffee and dessert. As one o'clock neared, Allison was nervous that she wouldn't be back in time for her three o'clock meeting with Brandon and Catherine about her ideas for the Project Fountain launch. And if this meeting went poorly, Allison knew she would not have much to say. Her future was riding on this meal, and the guest of honor was nowhere in sight.

Allison's attention was diverted to a commotion in the front of the restaurant. "You better damn well validate parking. It's bad enough that I had to hand over my Mercedes to some illegal immigrant, but don't make me pay for parking!"

Allison could immediately guess to whom the voice belonged; she saw the manager approach the irate man and assure him that parking would be taken care of. A minute later, the manager walked the irate man to the back of the restaurant, toward Allison's table. "Ms. Hart, your guest is here."

Allison stood to shake hands with her guest and offered her thanks to the restaurant's manager. He left them alone, and Allison and Stanley took their seats.

"Can you believe that, the nerve of them thinking I would pay for parking? Now how is it I have never heard of your name before?" Stanley asked. "A woman as beautiful as you should have been on my radar."

Nothing made Allison more upset than being placated by a chauvinist. Allison didn't want to be on anyone's radar screen because of her looks; she wanted her work to be what people thought of when they heard the name Allison Hart. Still, she had to play it cool because she knew how much was riding on this lunch. "You are too kind, Stanley. I am just an up-and-comer—I'm sure you could teach me a lot about how to make it in Tinseltown." Allison used the nickname for Hollywood that nobody, absolutely nobody, had used in the past 25 years, as a way of bonding with the Hollywood dinosaur.

"It's true," Stanley said, leaning in toward Allison. "Good old Stanley can teach you a thing or two about making it in Hollywood."

Allison bit her lip as he referred to himself in the third person; another one of her pet peeves. He was no better than T-Bang! What was it with the men in this town? "Tell me," Allison said, leaning in toward Stanley, "when did you first come to town? I want to hear all about it."

Allison leaned back, Stanley did the same, and she spent the next 15 minutes listening to Stanley recount how he'd grown up in an Irish neighborhood in Fairfield County, Connecticut, amidst plumbers and contractors. She suffered through his dreams of being a bigshot attorney, then bombing his LSATs and settling for a third-tier law school. He then admitted that he wound up an entertainment agent after moving to Hollywood and befriending Elizabeth Pierce. "I knew her biblically, as my parents would say."

"Wait a minute," Allison said. "You mean to tell me you became an agent after having an affair with Elizabeth Pierce from *Casa Grande?*"

"She had a thing for younger men, and apparently I was just her type. That show made my career."

Their conversation was interrupted by the arrival of their waiter. "I'm Marcus, your waiter today. Do you want to hear the specials?" Without waiting for a reply, Marcus began spouting off the specials, not making eye contact with either Allison or Stanley, as if his mind were elsewhere.

"A lady as lovely as you should order first," Stanley said to Allison.

Allison, biting her tongue, responded, "I'll have a Caesar salad with dressing on the side please."

"Any protein for your salad, ma'am?" Marcus asked.

"Some grilled shrimp, please," Allison replied.

"And for you, sir?" The waiter gestured in Stanley's general direction.

"I would like a hamburger, medium rare, with nothing but pickles on it."

"May I have your menus, please?" Marcus asked.

Allison and Stanley handed the waiter their menus and watched him saunter off toward the hostess.

Allison turned her attention to Stanley. "Do you believe in coincidences, Stanley?"

"Like when you think of a song and then it comes on the radio?" Stanley asked. "That happens to me all the time. I used to think I was psychic."

Allison thought to herself, *If a psychic ever told me I would one day be sitting across from an Irish person with a Jewish last name who claimed to be psychic, I would have punched her in the face and demanded my money back.* "I ask you that because I've put together a show idea that involves Elizabeth Pierce and the rest of the stars of *Casa Grande*, reuniting for a reunion of sorts."

It was clear that this piqued Stanley's interest, as his eyebrows lifted toward his toupee and his forehead scrunched. "What did you have in mind?"

Allison proceeded to summarize the idea that she, Lucy, and Bruce came up with: a show that would be a hybrid of popular reality formats, part voyeuristic and part competition. "We are even working on a way to answer the age-old question, *who stabbed Kyle Dixon?*"

"Maybe I'm a little thick, Ms. Hart, but what's the storyline?" Stanley knew that most reality shows employed writers and that what is perceived by the audience to be reality is really just another form of fiction.

"We've done our homework on these actors, Stanley. We've also talked to people who were involved in the show, and they assure us that getting them in a room together will lead to more exciting TV than anyone has seen in a while."

Stanley knew that the writers of *Casa Grande* could never have come up with storylines that were as colorful as what the cast was up to offscreen.

"What's my part in this?" Stanley asked. "Out of all those actors, the only one I represent is Blaze."

"We've tracked down Elizabeth, Vanessa, and Danny," Allison stated. "They are all interested in appearing on the show. We initially had some trouble locating Victor—apparently he escaped from the retirement home where was living—but we recently found him, living with Danny. He's open to doing the show, provided he won't be sent back to the home. The one person we have not been able to get in touch with about this opportunity is your client Blaze Hazelwood."

"Well," Stanley replied, "I'm not sure he would go for it. He doesn't approve of reality TV, and it's not like he needs the money."

"Let me show you something, Stanley." Allison reached into her bag, pulled out a piece of paper, and handed it to Stanley.

Stanley stared at the sheet of paper he was handed, looked at Allison, and said, "What exactly am I looking at here?"

Allison explained how her show *Bling It On* was distributed, that because it was online they had access to data that TV shows could not get. "The line chart on the top shows the number of people who have watched the stream of *Bling It On* since its inception. Take a look at the data for two Fridays ago."

"It looks as if there was a spike in the number of viewers watching," Stanley remarked. "What does the number below each date on the line graph show?"

"Those numbers represent the average number of times a viewer replayed an episode. Two weeks ago we saw our repeat viewing rate triple."

"So what happened two weeks ago?" Stanley asked.

"I thought you might ask that question," Allison said. "Take a look for yourself."

Allison handed Stanley a tablet computer, got up from her seat, and walked around behind his chair to look over his shoulder. It was clear that he didn't know what he was supposed to do with the device, so Allison reached over his shoulder, touched the screen, and hit Play.

Stanley began watching the scene between Blaze and T-Bang, and Allison returned to her seat. "That's what happened two weeks ago," Allison said. "Your client wandered onto our program and the Internet went crazy." After the clip finished, Allison handed Stanley another piece of paper.

"What's this?" Stanley asked.

"That," Allison replied, "is a report showing the most popular search terms on Google since Blaze wandered onto our show two weeks ago. The number-one searched term is Blaze Hazelwood, and the number two is *Casa Grande*. Blaze fever is beginning again, Stanley, and it's up to you and me to capitalize on it."

Before Allison could say anything else, Marcus was back with their food. "A Caesar salad with grilled shrimp for the lady and a hamburger with pickles for the gentleman. Is there anything else I can get for you?"

Allison and Stanley said no and dug in, resuming their conversation between bites.

"So how do you make money in reality TV anyway?" Stanley asked.

Allison proceeded to describe the revenue model she'd designed for the show; each actor would be compensated with a per-episode salary and shares of UPC stock. She added that the winner of the competition would become the face of a UPC brand and win a $1 million contract. "Their face will be all over TV, print, billboards, and online; you won't be able to go anywhere without seeing them."

"I think you have something here," Stanley admitted. "But Blaze will be tricky—unlike his fellow co-stars, he doesn't need the money. And he will resist the reality format."

"Okay," Allison said. "But if there's one thing I've learned about actors, it's that actors have to act. This opportunity will give your client the ability to be seen on the screen—that's got to be better than being a voice in a video game or in some kids' movie."

"I'm meeting him for dinner this evening," Stanley mentioned. "I'll run the idea by him then."

Allison nodded her agreement, and they were interrupted by Marcus. "Is there anything I can clear for you?" Marcus asked, picking up their plates before they had a chance to respond. "I hope you saved room for coffee and dessert."

Allison said, "Mint tea for me, please."

Stanley replied, "Crème brûlée for me please, along with a cappuccino.'"

Allison reached into her purse, pulled out a business card, and handed it to Stanley. "Please call me after your meeting with Blaze."

"Of course," Stanley replied.

With talk of business behind them, Allison and Stanley

waited for their drinks and dessert to arrive, and Stanley proceeded to tell Allison everything he felt she should know about Hollywood.

After signing off on the check at 2:45, Allison was nervous that she would be late for her meeting with Brandon and Catherine. After making sure that Stanley's parking was paid for, Allison said goodbye to her lunch guest and then walked briskly toward her office—but not too briskly. The last thing she wanted was to arrive all sweaty and out of breath; she knew that the Ice Queen would pounce on any sign of weakness.

As for Stanley, he got in his car and drove back to his condo in the valley. He knew that he had his work cut out for him getting Blaze interested in *Return to Casa Grande*, and he knew there was one person he could call for help. But it had been 25 years since they'd spoken, and he knew she was one to hold a grudge. Still, he knew the call could be the insurance policy he needed to ensure Blaze's return to *Casa Grande*.

CHAPTER SEVENTEEN

Return to Casa Grande

Allison made it back for her meeting with Brandon and Catherine with five minutes to spare. She checked in with Margo, Brandon's assistant, who informed her that Brandon was just finishing up his lunch meeting with Catherine and to have a seat.

Just then Margo's phone buzzed; it was Brandon instructing Margo to send Allison in. Allison stood up, took a deep breath, and walked through the door.

"Allison, good to see you. Catherine and I are excited to see what you're going to share with us today."

Allison looked around the room. "Where's Catherine?"

"Over here, darling," Catherine replied, exiting Brandon's private bathroom. "I just had to powder my nose."

"Why don't we all have a seat," Brandon said, and they sat down at the round conference table in the corner of Brandon's office.

Catherine placed her hands on her knees, looked Allison directly in the eyes, and let the silence hang over the table for several uncomfortable seconds. "What have you come up with for Project Fountain?"

Allison was careful not to let her intimidation show. She folded her hands, placed them on her knees, and looked Catherine in the eye. "We've sketched out something we believe will work well for the launch of Project Fountain. It's a page out of the Bling It On playbook but focuses on personalities that are more in line with the Project Fountain target." Allison then paused and waited for some sign of interest from Brandon and Catherine, who just stared at her. No matter how cool Allison tried to play it, they could play it cooler.

"The concept is entitled Return to Casa Grande and will focus on—"

Catherine jumped in, "Casa Grande, as in the '80s soap Casa Grande?"

"The same," Allison replied.

"No way," Brandon said immediately. "I'm not going to have the Believe brand cheapened by aging soap stars."

Catherine intervened, "Brandon, you haven't even heard the idea yet; give Allison a chance to pitch it before you make up your mind."

"What is there to hear? How is following around a bunch of has-been actors going to give the brand the exposure it needs for a successful launch?"

Allison was determined not to let Brandon get the best of her. She was perplexed by Catherine's support; she had assumed Catherine would pose the greater resistance. For the second time that day, Allison painted the broad strokes of the idea that she, Lucy, and Bruce had created for the show.

"How does the brand tie in?" Brandon asked.

"Each of these personalities is trying to remain relevant in Hollywood. Elizabeth Pierce and Vanessa Crestwood are broke and need to find work immediately. Danny Maieye had an altercation with his most recent employer, the Roman Catholic Church, and is now living in Victor Tillmans' apartment. Victor himself just escaped from the retirement home his family put him in a few years back. Even Blaze Hazelwood, who managed to maintain a semblance of a career, is looking to move from voiceover work and fan appearances to 'real' acting. Each of these people has one thing in common: Their age is working against them. We all know Hollywood isn't an equal opportunity employer. They need to look younger to find work, so the positioning of Project Fountain is a nice fit."

"The logic is sound," Brandon admitted. "But how do we know anyone still cares about these people?"

Allison reached into her bag and handed Catherine and Brandon the same tablet computer she'd shown Stanley at their lunch. "Just hit Play."

Catherine and Brandon watched the altercation between Blaze and T-Bang and put the tablet down. "What was that?" Brandon asked.

"Well, he's certainly held up well!" Catherine said.

"Who?" Brandon asked, a note of anger in his voice. "Will one of you please tell me what I just watched?"

"That, my dear Brandon," Catherine said, "was Blaze Hazelwood. He somehow managed to walk onto Allison's little reality show."

"Blaze Hazel-who?" Brandon asked.

"Wood," Catherine replied, and thought to herself, *Wood, indeed! He's hardly aged at all, and oh, my, that bulge!*

Allison slid some papers across the table, and Catherine

pulled her attention back to the room. "Take a look at this report," Allison said. "The feed of *Bling It On* where Blaze confronts T-Bang is the most-watched and most-shared feed of all; the Lust team is ecstatic."

"What was the general market response?" Brandon asked.

Allison handed over another report. "Blaze Hazelwood was the most often-searched term on Google for three days following that altercation. I called a friend at Netflix, and she said they have been inundated with requests to start streaming *Casa Grande*. It seems the country has Blaze fever, and I think we should capitalize on it."

Brandon asked the next logical question, "So have you approached anyone in the cast about your idea?"

"We have just about everyone on board with verbal interest," Allison replied.

"Everyone but whom?" Catherine asked.

"We have some issues to work out with Victor Tillmans."

"What kind of issues?" Brandon asked.

"I mentioned before that he escaped from the retirement home he was living in," Allison said. "He's currently going around town dressed as Marilyn Monroe, to avoid being caught and sent back there. He will only do the show on the condition that he not have to return to Shady Acres. As such, he is demanding that he be allowed to do the show dressed as Marilyn Monroe."

"Victor isn't who I'm concerned about," Catherine replied. "Is Blaze on board yet?"

"I've just come from lunch with his agent," Allison responded. "He's going to present the idea to Blaze this evening. He warned me, though, that the reality angle may be a turnoff for Blaze, as he doesn't think highly of the genre."

"Let me make one thing crystal clear for you," Catherine said coldly. "No Blaze, no show."

Brandon interrupted, "If Blaze is meeting with his agent tonight, let's regroup tomorrow morning for an update. If the news is bad, we'll have to come up with a plan B quickly. We only have a few months to go before our launch, and for this to be right, the show will need to be ready to air by then."

"That's the beauty of this format," Allison said. "The fact that it's unscripted saves us a bunch of time."

They agreed to meet the next morning at 10 and all stood up and walked toward the door, where they said their goodbyes. Allison noticed something peculiar as Catherine shook her hand goodbye: She was missing an earring. She filed the tidbit in the back of her mind, along with Catherine's reaction to seeing Blaze Hazelwood on the recording. *Why was she blushing?*

On the way to her office she called Marios and asked him to gather up Bruce and Lucy for an all-nighter later that evening, so they could start working on a plan B. She also asked her assistant to arrange a meeting for her and the head of UPC's security services, as she'd heard that they were working on video capture technology that might be able to capture every moment of the show in a very inconspicuous way.

Given that the fate of her show rested in the ability of a third-rate agent to convince a second-rate actor about a first-rate opportunity, she felt slightly out of control, and if there was one thing she hated, it was not feeling in control.

Upon reaching her office, Allison was handed a stack of notes from Marios, along with a package. "Looks like you got something, girlfriend," Marios said sassily. "Secret admirer?"

Allison looked at the return address; it was marked TVSN. Allison thought to herself, *Thank goodness it's here.* When Allison felt out of control, the only thing that would make her feel relaxed was some private time. Since she didn't currently have a man in her life, "private time" consisted of a long bath, a glass of wine, and a waterproof toy (or two) to help her relax—none of which were available to her at the office. Allison instructed her assistant to hold all calls and make sure she remained undisturbed for the next hour, as she had a lot of "thinking" to do.

Allison entered her office, locked the door, and rushed to her desk, where she found a letter opener and opened the box. A minute later she was holding her very own Vibratoe in her hands. *I can't believe I bought this*, she thought to herself. *But sometimes a girl has to take matters into her own hands.* With the Vibratoe in hand, Allison turned off the lights, walked to her couch, and began to "relax." She put her new best friend on its third and most intense setting, "toegasm," because she didn't have a moment to waste.

CHAPTER EIGHTEEN
An Unfocused Group

Blaze was in a group of strangers, pretending to be Peter James—a 65-year-old male suffering from a prostate condition known as benign prostatic hyperplasia, or BPH for short—discussing his opinions on a drug to treat an enlarged prostate, when his mobile phone rang for the first time. He loved patient-centered focus groups because they gave him a chance to display a range of emotions that your average focus group simply could not provide. He ignored his vibrating phone while telling the group, "The worst part about it is the frequency of urination, particularly late at night; my wife wonders why I am always going to the bathroom in the middle of the night. She just doesn't get it."

The other men participating in the group met this last comment with nods of approval.

Blaze looked down at his phone and saw that it was ringing a third time. The caller ID read "My Fat Agent."

Blaze announced to the group, "It's my doctor, with the results of my biopsy. Please excuse me." He picked up his bag and left the room. As soon as he was outside he answered the phone. "Stanley, how many times do I have to fucking tell you, if I don't answer my phone right away just leave a message. Or better yet, learn how to text."

"Blaze, babe, I'm 55 years old and my fingers are too fat for texting. And I don't trust that you actually receive the messages I leave on your answering machine because you never call me back. Maybe you gotta change the tape or something."

"It's called voicemail, Stanley, and I do get your messages. I just choose not to call you back since you never have anything serious for me."

"Hey, is that a way to treat the guy who made you the voice of Saturday evening cartoons? I'm just calling to make sure we're still on for dinner tonight in Beverly Hills. I have two ideas to pitch to you."

"Yeah, we're still on. I'm in Westwood now and should be able to get there by six."

"Wonderful, see you—" Blaze had ended the call.

Blaze walked back into the room and sat down. He managed to produce a tear, which was on its way down his cheek just as the moderator asked, "Is everything alright, Peter?"

Blaze announced to the group that his test had come back negative, and everyone in the group began to clap their hands for him.

CHAPTER NINETEEN
Stanley's Insurance Policy

Stanley was pacing back and forth, waiting for his phone to ring; he had left a message for Elizabeth Pierce immediately after his lunch with Allison and he had yet to hear back from her. Stanley was nervous that Blaze would say no to *Return to Casa Grande* and he was afraid his future in Hollywood depended on a yes from his client. The divorce settlements to his first and second wives were bleeding him dry and he needed this deal. That's where Elizabeth Pierce came in; if there was anyone who had dirt on Blaze that Stanley could use to his advantage, it would be Elizabeth—she had dirt on everyone.

The silence in his home was broken by the ringing of his wall-mounted phone, an old rotary model without caller ID. Stanley silently prayed that it wasn't someone looking to sell him solar panels. He picked up the phone and answered with his trademark response, "Roth."

"I know you're not," said an older woman's crackly voice. "You were the first Irishman I ever had, darling, and oh, what fun I had teaching you about how

95

Hollywood really works."

"Elizabeth, thank you for returning my call, it's been far too long. It's so good to hear your—"

"Cut the bullshit, Stanley, and tell me why all of a sudden a voice from my past—which I have not heard in 25 years, mind you—reaches out to me, sounding desperate."

Stanley thought it sounded like she was slurring her words a bit and worried that she had started drinking again. What did he know? Maybe she never stopped. "I've just had a meeting with Allison Hart," Stanley said. "I believe you know her."

"Ahh, yes, that little girl of a woman looking to bring back the stars of *Casa Grande*. I spoke with her earlier this week and am even entertaining doing it. Why?"

"There's a wild card: Hazelwood. If he doesn't agree to do the show, it's not going to happen. So as you can see it is in both of our best interests to get Blaze to see the light."

Elizabeth was quiet for a minute. "I just might have something you can use to lock down Blaze. It's a long shot, but it may work."

"I'm all ears," Stanley said.

Upon hearing that, Elizabeth told Stanley a secret that she had kept for more than a quarter of a century, a secret that now only four people on the planet were privy to.

"Well, thank you for being a friend!" Stanley exclaimed after being let in on the secret that, if exposed, would certainly hinder Blaze's future in Hollywood. "Mind you, I am thoroughly disgusted by this knowledge and will likely have trouble eating tonight, but I agree it may be just what we need to win over Blaze. You're sure that you still have the Polaroids?"

"In my safe deposit box, darling," Elizabeth said. "And don't be so quick to judge, Stanley, not all the women you've bedded have been supermodels."

Stanley agreed and thanked Elizabeth for her time, hung up the phone, and then made a beeline for the shower with a new spring in his step. He wanted to look his best for his dinner with Blaze, but he also wanted to cleanse himself of the knowledge that had just been imparted to him by Elizabeth. *I knew he had a thing for older women*, Stanley thought to himself, *but that was wrong on so many levels.*

CHAPTER TWENTY
50 Shades of Clay

Blaze didn't have time to go home and transform himself from a 65-year-old khakis-wearing enlarged prostate patient to 45-year-old television star Blaze Hazelwood, so he had to do so at Equifit, the high-end gym he belonged to in Beverly Hills. He always kept a stash of evening clothes in his locker at the gym, as going back and forth to his home in Malibu was not practical, particularly during rush hour.

Blaze knew he was going to be a few minutes early for dinner and that Stanley was going to be a few minutes late. Since he hated sitting at a table alone, Blaze opted to have a seat at the bar while he waited for Stanley to arrive. It had been a while since he had been to Pate's, but the place looked exactly the same as it had when it opened in 1954. With its dark lighting, blood-red carpeting, and leather booths, walking into Pate's was like walking through a time warp; it was as much a dinosaur of Hollywood as his agent was.

The bartender recognized Blaze immediately. "No

fraulein with you tonight, Mr. Hazelwood?" This particular bartender knew about Blaze's reputation in Germany and never failed to comment on it.

"Not tonight, I'm afraid, Lloyd," Blaze said with a little disappointment in his voice. "Tonight's dinner is strictly business."

"Just remember, Mr. Hazelwood, all work and no play makes Blaze a dull boy." Lloyd delivered that line using his best Jack Nicholson impersonation—which sounded more like Ethel Merman.

"Keep on practicing that voice," Blaze said, "and you won't be tending bar here much longer."

"You're too kind, Mr. Hazelwood," Lloyd said. "Tonight you are lucky, we just received another case of Zima imported from Japan. Would you like me to pour you a Zima over ice with a drop of grenadine?" This made Blaze happy. He truly cherished an ice-cold Zima, a carbonated alcoholic beverage popular in the 1990s but no longer available for sale in the States. It was still marketed in Japan and thus had to be imported.

"Lloyd, you just made my day. But please put it in a martini glass."

Blaze took a sip of his drink, closed his eyes, and felt a sense of calmness come over his body. The serenity of the moment died, however, when he heard a commotion behind him and knew, without having to turn around, that Stanley had arrived. Blaze looked over his shoulder and saw his overweight agent with his bad toupee arguing with a red-headed hostess, but was too far away to hear what the argument was about.

"Thank you, Lloyd," Blaze said, leaving a twenty on the bar. He walked toward the front of the restaurant, where

Stanley was causing a scene. Once Blaze got a little bit closer, he heard the hostess say, "Yes, we do validate parking, but only for guests whose bill is greater than $300."

Blaze interrupted, "You'll have to excuse my friend, luv." He turned on his charm along with his British affectation in an attempt to diffuse the situation; he also found the hostess extremely attractive. He winked at her. "He is clearly suffering from some head trauma," he said, pointing toward Stanley's toupee. "Apologies again for my friend here. Let me make it up to you by buying you a drink after your shift ends."

"Let me show you to your table," she said. "Ernesto will be your server tonight and he will be with you shortly." She blew Blaze a kiss when Stanley wasn't looking and whispered, "Come find me when you leave."

"Thanks, luv," Blaze said.

"What is it with you and this 'luv' business? Since when did you become an English gentleman?"

"Since when did you become Jewish?" Blaze countered. "Did I ever tell you that my grandparents on my mother's side were Eastern European Jews who escaped the Holocaust?"

"Once or twice," said Stanley.

"How do you think they would feel if they knew my agent is an Irish lad from Connecticut who changed his name to Stanley Roth for 'professional reasons'?" Blaze put "professional reasons" in air quotes.

"All I'm saying is that you always seem to be playing a character. I don't think the world knows who the real Blaze Hazelwood is."

"The world," Blaze said, pausing only to wink at the

hostess, who he'd caught staring at him, "isn't ready for the real Blaze Hazelwood."

Their conversation was interrupted by the arrival of Ernesto, their waiter. "Good evening, gentlemen...oh my Gawd, you are Blaze Hazelwood, aren't you?" Like many gay men of his age, Ernesto grew up watching *Casa Grande* and had a crush on Blaze.

"In the flesh, luv," Blaze replied with his British affectation.

"Are we celebrating anything special tonight? New role?"

Blaze was pleased with the attention from Ernesto. "Well, I am waiting to see what Stanley over here has to say."

"We are celebrating the anniversary of Blaze's affair with a German pop star's mother."

"That was a long time ago, Stanley," Blaze argued.

"Memories live on in this town," Stanley fired back.

Sensing he needed to take a drink order, Ernesto asked, "Would you two like any water to start? Perhaps a bottle of Per—"

Stanley blurted, "Tap water will be fine."

"And how about something a little stronger, would you like a wine list?"

"Stanley here will have a glass of your house merlot, and I'll have another Zima with a dash of grenadine."

Sensing that this table would not run up a big bill, and therefore not provide a sizable tip, Ernesto walked away frustrated, "Would you like me to resurrect the Gin Blossoms as well?" Ernesto muttered under his breath and trotted away toward the bar to enter their drink orders.

"So, Blaze, how did your focus group go the other

day?"

"Since you asked." Blaze took his phone out of his pocket and found a picture of the teacher he took home after the focus group.

"That's better than that Lola you took home a few nights ago."

"She was an English teacher and she tickled my Longfellow, if you know what I mean."

Ernesto arrived with their drinks. "A glass of house merlot for the fatty and Zima for the hottie. Would you like to hear some of our specials tonight?"

"Not necessary," Stanley introjected. "Blaze, why don't you go ahead and order first."

Blaze looked over at the hostess as he said, "I'll have the red snapper."

"And for you, sir?" Ernesto asked Stanley.

"Caesar salad to start, but please put the dressing on the side, and for my main meal I'll have the steak tidbits."

"Would you like an itty-bitty bib for that?" Ernesto muttered under his breath while he was writing the order down.

"Pardon me?" said Stanley.

"I asked how you would like them cooked?" replied the waiter.

"Medium, please, and could I get fries instead of a baked potato?"

"Anything for you, Sir Spends-a-Lot."

Before Stanley could reply, Ernesto was off prancing toward the kitchen to place their order.

"That guy has some nerve!" Stanley said.

"Stanley," Blaze replied, "we are in LA. Every waiter in every restaurant is trying to be an actor and feels they are too good to be waiting tables. Little do they know, if they ever hit it big they just might miss these days."

"Let's get down to business. I have a few exciting things to chat about with you. Have you ever heard of the book *Fifty Shades of Grey?*"

"Read it cover to cover," Blaze admitted. "As I did the two sequels."

"Well, that is good news indeed," Stanley said with a wink. "They're making a movie—"

"No fucking way, you got me an audition for Christian Grey?"

"Clay," Stanley corrected his client. "Christian Clay."

Blaze looked confused. "No, his name is Christian Grey. Like I said, I read all the books."

"Have you ever watched Cinemax after midnight?"

"Yes, of course, Skinemax," Blaze said, referring to the network's nickname, because of the soft-core porn it aired after hours. "Why are you changing the subject on me?"

"Well, someone over at Cinemax wants to do a late-night parody called *Fifty Shades of Clay* and they want you to be the voice of the claymation version of Christian Grey."

Blaze just stared at Stanley in disbelief.

"Blaze," Stanley said, "tell me what is more realistic, Hollywood coming to an actor who has not been on the big screen in over 20 years to play the lead role in a feature film based on the biggest-selling book of the past few years, or a second-tier cable network coming to the same actor to voice a character in a parody of one of the biggest-selling books of the past few years?"

"Way to lift my spirits, Stanley. Who did you learn your bedside manner from, Dr. Mengele?"

"Hey, this voiceover work pays the bills."

"But I want to be seen again!" Blaze shouted, pounding his fist on the table. "I don't want to play another fucking pony or a claymation figurine with a hard-on and a ball gag!"

Stanley saw his opening. "Blaze, remember a few weeks ago when you sauntered over to your neighbor's house and wound up on his reality show?"

"Yeah, so?" Blaze replied.

"Do you remember what happened the next day? The Twitternet almost broke."

"Yes, I remember."

"Well, something has come up," Stanley said, "and it's a big opportunity for you to get right back into the limelight."

Blaze's eyes went wide with anticipation; the thought of being back in the public eye was causing his mouth to water. "I'm listening," said Blaze. "What is it?"

Stanley took a deep breath, flashed a big smile, and said *"Return to Casa Grande."*

Blaze let the words ring in his ear for a minute. "What is it, some kind of reunion show? Or does the network want to reboot the show with a new cast?"

"None of the above," Stanley said.

Blaze stared at his agent. "Well, then, what is it?"

Stanley remained silent and started fidgeting in his chair. All eye contact between them, gone.

And then the pieces came together in Blaze's head. "No way. No fucking way. There is no fucking way my agent who I've been with for over 25 years is sitting here talking to me about doing a reality TV show. Have you taken to sniffing the glue that holds that rug on your head?"

The volume of Blaze's voice had attracted the attention of the surrounding diners. "Blaze," Stanley said, "please try to keep your voice down. Let me explain."

"What is there to explain?" Blaze said. "All I see when I turn on the television is 'reality' TV, and there is nothing real about it!" To accentuate his point, Blaze put the word "reality" in air quotes. "Those shows are clearly scripted, and scripted poorly, I might add. To top it off, the 'stars' of these shows are not there because of their talent— they're there because of their outrageous behavior. There is no art to their 'craft,'" Blaze argued, putting "craft" in air quotes. "I won't do it. I won't stoop that low!"

"Will you please allow me to at least tell you the premise?" Stanley pleaded.

Blaze sat glaring at Stanley with his arms crossed across his chest.

"The original cast returns to the mansion near Malibu where the exteriors of the show were shot, and you all live in the mansion and all of your interactions are filmed. No script whatsoever."

"Who the hell would want to watch that?" Blaze asked. "And who the hell would want to sponsor that?"

"You saw what happened after you made your surprise appearance on T-Bang's show," Stanley argued. "The country went wild. You awakened a sleeping giant that had been dormant for over two decades. As for a sponsor, that's the beauty of it: the idea for the show came from the sponsor."

"Who is the sponsor?"

"Believe!" Stanley replied.

"I've been in this town so long I don't believe anything. Why should I start now?"

"No, Blaze, you don't understand. Believe is one of the biggest skin care brands in the world—it made its parent company over two billion dollars last year. They about to launch the biggest line extension in company history and want to do so using *Return to Casa Grande* as a launch vehicle.

Most actors would not know what a launch vehicle is for a marketing campaign, but Blaze had participated in enough focus groups to understand that companies did all sorts of things to launch a product, including entertainment tie-ins. "Have the others been approached yet?" Blaze asked.

Stanley didn't miss a beat. "Vanessa, Elizabeth, and Danny are all in, and we are working out the details for Victor but are confident we can get that solved. The only one missing is you. Blaze, consider this: You're already a star who has proven himself—you're not turning to reality TV to make you famous. And who knows where this will go? What's the worst that could happen?"

"Famous last words, Stanley," Blaze said dejectedly.

Stanley could see that Blaze was considering the show; he didn't want to break out the secret weapon Elizabeth had given him if he didn't have to. It could, after all, lead to Blaze storming out of the restaurant and the end of their relationship. Just thinking about the details that Elizabeth had shared with him was enough to have him question his appetite.

"I'll take a meeting with the producers. That's all I will commit to right now," Blaze said. "If I like what they have to say, I'll consider it. If I don't, I walk. Is that understood?"

"Crystal clear," Stanley said. "Let me ring them now."

Instead of reaching into his jacket pocket and pulling out a phone, Stanley called for the waiter to come to the table.

"Your gourmet plate of steak tidbits and French fries will be out momentarily, sir. We are just preparing a fresh ketchup reduction sauce for your dipping pleasure now."

"That's not why I called you over here; can you bring a phone to this table?"

For once Ernesto was at a loss for words, "Do you need to borrow a cell phone?" Ernesto was so perplexed by the request, he dropped the fake Italian accent he had been using.

"Stanley," Blaze said, "Just use my phone." Blaze handed Stanley his iPhone and Stanley just looked at it blankly for a good sixty seconds.

"You don't know how to use it, do you?" Blaze asked.

"Who am I, Scotty from *Star Trek*?" Stanley retorted.

"What's the number?"

"I was going to call information to get it."

Blaze shook his head. "What's the name and where do they work?"

"Allison Hart," Stanley replied. "And she works at the Universal Products Company."

A few seconds later, Blaze had her number up on his screen. He handed the phone back to Stanley after it had started dialing.

"What do I do with this now?" Stanley asked.

"Try putting it up to your ear," Blaze said. "When you hear the other person pick up, say hello." Blaze had put the phone on speaker, so he could hear the exchange.

"Allison Hart's office, Marios speaking. How can I help you?"

"Allison Hart, please."

"And who might I say is calling?"

"Stanley Roth; she's expecting my call."

"Just one moment and I'll put you through."

"Allison Hart."

"Allison, it's me, Stanley."

"Is it good news or bad news, Stanley?"

"I'm sitting with him right now. He didn't say yes, but he didn't say no. He wants to have a meeting with you to discuss it further."

"Okay, set it up for tomorrow if possible. Just call Marios—I'll shift around anything I need to in order to meet with Blaze."

"Will do."

"She sounds cute," Blaze said.

"It's funny you say that," Stanley mentioned. "When I met her there was something about her that immediately reminded me of you. Can you make tomorrow work?"

"The only thing I have going on tomorrow is two hours of recording for an episode of *Family Guy*; they are doing a cutaway scene featuring *Back to the Future: The Musical* and want me to be the voice of Marty."

They were interrupted by Ernesto delivering their food to the table. "Enjoy your meal, gentlemen."

The rest of their meal went smoothly and both turned down dessert much to the chagrin of Ernesto. Stanley paid the bill while Blaze sauntered over to the hostess with the flaming red hair and paid for his valet parking as well as Stanley's. "So what is your name anyway?"

"Holly."

"Holly. Well, that's a pretty name. Tell me, would you like me to put the 'wood' back in Hollywood?"

"Mmm, you're a bad boy, aren't you, Mr. Hazelwood?"

"How did you know my name?" Blaze asked.

"*Bling It On* is my favorite show—I recognized you from the moment you sat at the bar. I don't finish here until 11:30," Holly said. "But if you can wait, there is a cool place called Jones where a lot of rock guys hang out. I hear T-Bang is supposed to be there tonight; maybe we can be on his show."

"Maybe, luv," Blaze said, not sure whether to laugh or cry.

"How was your red snapper?" she asked.

"Very tender," Blaze said. "And not the least bit fishy."

"Come get me at 11:30," Holly said, "and later you might get some snapper like you've never had."

"11:30 it is, luv," Blaze said.

He returned to the table to gather up his agent. Stanley asked, "Are you ever going to grow up, Blaze? Doesn't that ever get old?"

"What, picking up beautiful women and having brief, noncommittal physical relationships with them? What could possibly get old about that?"

CHAPTER TWENTY-ONE

Danny's Ghosts come back to Haunt

Danny was in the waiting room of the monsignor's office, feeling as uncomfortable as he had ever felt in his life. This feeling was not improved by the interaction he was having with the monsignor's assistant, Mary.

"I for one think they should let you guys get married," she offered out of the blue. "Who can blame a handsome guy like you for wanting a little pleasure of the flesh?"

"I didn't pursue that woman," Daniel said wearily.

"Look, Father Daniel, I've been in this job for a long time, and you wouldn't be the first priest the monsignor had to reprimand for breaking a vow of chastity. Frankly, I don't know how you guys even entertain the notion; if my husband doesn't get the marital embrace at least three times a week he's climbing the walls."

By this point, Father Daniel was too exhausted to defend himself any further and simply replied with a long sigh. The phone on Mary's desk buzzed, she picked up and simply said, "Okay."

"Is he ready for me?" Father Daniel asked.

"Good luck, Father. He doesn't sound like he's in a great mood."

Father Daniel replied with, "Thanks for the pep talk," and then stood up and went into the monsignor's office.

The monsignor was seated at his desk with the remnants of his dinner still on his mouth and his clerical garb. Without even bothering to swallow his last bite, he said, "Have a seat, Daniel."

"Thank you, Monsignor Hewson."

"We've concluded our investigation into your behavior, Father Daniel, and frankly it doesn't look good for you." He let those words hang in the air for a few minutes before continuing. "Is there anything you would like to confess to me?"

"Monsignor Hewson, I can say with an honest heart and a clear conscience that I did not approach that woman in the confessional—she approached me."

The monsignor handed Daniel a manila envelope and said, "Father Daniel, if there is one thing I despise, it's a liar."

"What's this?"

"Open it and take a look."

Father Daniel opened the envelope and saw screenshots of what appeared to be a text message exchange between himself and the choir director, clearly doctored. Of most concern were messages that appeared to show sexting between the two, and pictures that he supposedly had sent her, of him in various states of undress—but they were pictures taken long before he'd become a priest.

"What do you have to say for yourself?" the monsignor asked.

"Someone has doctored those pictures up!" Danny

exclaimed. "Those pictures were taken over ten years ago. I have no idea how they would have gotten on her phone."

"It's clear to me that there are two possibilities: you are either delusional, or you're lying to me. Either way, the action I take remains the same. You are formally stripped of your duties as a priest. I should have listened to my misgivings about you 10 years ago when you were a seminarian."

"Monsignor, if I could just say something," Father Daniel pleaded.

"You have said enough. Now go on and leave before I have to call security."

The monsignor didn't bother to stand when Father Daniel, now just Daniel, stood up to leave.

"How did it go, Father?" Mary asked Daniel when he exited the monsignor's office. Too shocked to say anything, Daniel simply staggered out of the office.

#

Victor Tillmans was alone in his Culver City apartment when Danny came back from his meeting.

"So," Victor said, "how did it go with the pope?"

"Monsignor," Danny said disdainfully, "and it didn't go well. You are looking at the first priest to be defrocked from the diocese of Los Angeles in over five years. I don't know what I'm going to do now."

"Danny boy, did you ever think for a minute that someone set you up?"

"Of course the thought crossed my mind," Danny admitted, "but who would want to do such a thing?"

"Face the facts, kid, you upset a lot of ladies back in the day. I'm sure if you thought about it you could come up with a long list of possibilities. Hey, it's a good thing that show came along; now you can make a few bucks. Who knows, maybe it will get you back into acting!"

"Believe me," Danny said, "the last thing I want to do is embarrass myself on national TV. But you're right, what other choice do I have?"

"Listen, kid, I know you're going through a tough time right now, but what do you say we celebrate your newfound freedom tonight? How about we go to that place in Hollywood where you, me, and Blaze used to hang out. What was it called again?"

"Back then it was called Vertigo," Danny said. "I have no idea what it is now. But wait, you're not still afraid of getting caught and sent back to the retirement home?"

"The last place they would be looking for me is at a nightclub," Victor said. "But just to be on the safe side, maybe I should go as Marilyn. It's strange, but dressing like her feels so natural to me."

"To each their own," Danny said. He took out his phone and searched Google to see if Vertigo was still open. "Well, that's appropriate."

"What's that, kid?"

"The name of the club. It isn't Vertigo anymore; the new name is Penance."

"Alright, kid, lets change out of these threads, go to Penance, and say ten Hail Marys."

#

Vanessa Crestwood hung up the phone and immediately walked over to her kitchen counter where her purse was and found her pack of cigarettes. She removed one from the box, tapped it against her thigh, put it to her mouth and lit it. She savored both the flavor of the cigarette and the warmth it caused in her lungs on that first inhale. Her nerves were finally starting to calm down.

The call she just took was from her source inside the monsignor's office, who confirmed that Danny was relieved of his priestly duties. She had been feeling conflicted over the past few weeks about what she was doing to her old friend and former lover. It's true she held a grudge against him over how he ended their relationship and that she wanted to see him suffer, but she never intended for it to go this far. Kathleen Guilard, the choir director who made advances toward then-Father Daniel was an old friend of Vanessa's. Vanessa convinced her to flirt with Danny in exchange for a promise to introduce Kathleen to some "big-time agents." Kathleen, a struggling singer who took the job at the church not as a matter of faith but rather to help pay the bills, couldn't resist.

It wasn't to go further than flirting until the chance to do *Return to Casa Grande* came up. After seeing him preside over a mass at Our Lady of the Hills, Vanessa knew that Danny would never leave his priestly vocation behind to do the show, so she had to up the ante. She convinced Kathleen to approach Danny in the confessional and arranged for some old pictures of Danny to make their way to the monsignor's office. Now that he was a man without a home, he would have no choice but to sign on. That left only one holdout, Blaze Hazelwood.

CHAPTER TWENTY-TWO

Penance

It was only 9:30 and Blaze had two hours to kill before picking up Holly back at the restaurant, so he decided to take a drive to Penance, his favorite club in Hollywood. If there was one thing Blaze couldn't stand, it was being alone with his thoughts.

Penance had been known by a few different names over the past 30 years, but to the clubbers of the 1980s it would always be remembered as Vertigo—a club where on any given night you could see a who's who of celebrities. And it was the place where a 15-year-old Blaze Hazelwood lost his virginity, in a private VIP room, to a woman more than four times his age. To make it worse, his co-star Elizabeth Pierce had been there and taken Polaroids of Blaze and his seducer. It was a traumatic experience for the young Blaze, leaving him confused and ashamed, and he struggled to shake off that memory as he entered the club.

On the ground floor was a large dance floor playing current dance music. The second floor had two smaller theme rooms: a '70s room playing disco music and an '80s room playing new wave music, which Blaze thought ought to be called "old wave" now. The third floor had a number of private rooms that could be rented by the hour, which came with their own private cocktail waitress. The basement housed an almost pitch-black room decorated as a dungeon and was open to anyone who was into S&M.

Blaze walked up the stairs and found his way to the '80s room. It struck him that 25 years ago he would have been accosted on his ascent up the stairs, but tonight not one person asked for his autograph. Back then he had begged people to leave him alone; now that they did, he felt a longing for the days when he was in the limelight.

Walking into the '80s room, he noticed that no one was dancing. In the corner were a microphone and some speakers standing on tripods. "Holy fucking hell," Blaze mumbled to himself, "it's fucking karaoke night." The room was dark, but he looked around and noticed, at the bar, a sad sack of a man about Blaze's age, drowning his sorrows in a glass of whiskey, accompanied by an old woman dressed up as Marilyn Monroe. Just as he was turning to leave, he saw a rather attractive woman about twenty years his junior enter the room; she was followed by three equally young-looking friends, providing Blaze with the motivation to remain in the room a little longer.

"Ladies and gentlemen, thank you for your patience," said a radio-quality voice booming through the speakers in the front of the room. "My name is Johnny Wildman and I'm your host for '80s karaoke tonight here at Penance. Given it is a Friday night and we are going to turn up the heat in here, I bet more than a few of you will be in need of some penance by Sunday morning, am I right?"

Blaze noticed the four ladies putting their hands above their heads and screaming after the DJ finished speaking. They appeared to be intoxicated. He decided it was time to make his move.

"Next up, we have"—the DJ took a minute to comprehend what was written on his paper—"it looks like we have someone named Father Danny ready to do the 1985 Simple Minds classic 'Don't You Forget About Me.' Ladies and gentlemen, please put your hands together for Father Danny."

The crowd unenthusiastically did as they were told. Blaze noticed something familiar in the man who stumbled up onto the stage. He turned to one of the ladies next to him. "'Allo, luv," Blaze said with his British affectation. "Looks like this Father Danny over here had a little too much church wine." Blaze waited a few seconds, expecting a laugh out of the young woman but did not receive one; nothing bothered Blaze more than when his attempts at humor went unappreciated by a woman he had his eye on.

All eyes were on the singer at this point, who pointed drunkenly to the crowd and said, "Ladies and gentlemen of the diocese of LA, don't you forget about me." Then came the unmistakable drum beat and two-chord guitar opening, followed by "Hey hey hey hey ohhh…" For the next four minutes and twenty seconds everyone in the room watched in amazement while Danny sung every note perfectly and danced as if he were an original member of the band.

When the song was over everyone in the room, including Blaze, erupted with applause. "Thank you, everyone," the singer slurred. "My name is Danny Boy, and I'm back."

Blaze was in shock; he couldn't believe he hadn't recognized his old friend and costar Danny Boy but wondered if he remembered Stanley correctly when he mentioned that Danny had become a priest. If that were the case, Blaze wondered why he was doing '80s karaoke at a club in LA.

Danny caught his eye and gave a wink, then shouted from the stage, "Ladies and gentlemen, please put your hands together for my old friend Blaze fucking Hazelwood."

The girl next to Blaze turned to her friend and said, "Blaze fucking Hazel who?"

"Wood, luv," Blaze replied sharply and headed for the stage.

Daniel leaned toward him and said, "How about we do a song together for old times' sake, Blazey boy?" In the mid-'80s, before Danny's band Sinner's Swing became a headlining act, Blaze would often play rhythm guitar and sing backup vocals with Danny at smaller club dates. They could play any Van Halen album cover to cover.

"Not feeling it tonight, Danny old boy," Blaze replied. Danny hopped down off the stage and gave Blaze a hug. "Hey, why don't we go somewhere where we can actually hear each other? Let's get a room upstairs."

"Okay," Danny said, "except money is tight for me at the moment. Would you mind picking up the tab for the room?"

"Not a problem. Why don't you say goodbye to Scarilyn Monroe over there. Unless my eyes are deceiving me, she looks more like a man than a woman."

"That's because she is a he, and he is with me."

"We did some weird shit in the '80s, Danny, but nothing as weird as that!"

"You haven't heard, have you?"

"Heard what?" Blaze asked.

"We have a lot to catch up on," Danny said to Blaze and headed over to Victor. "Hey, Victoria, change of plans. We're going upstairs."

Victor got off his bar stool and walked over to his former protégés. Turning his attention to Blaze, Victor said, "Hey, kid."

Blaze recognized Victor immediately. "Victor—oh Christ! How long has it been, 25 years? But why the fuck are you dressed like a woman? You were the manliest man I ever knew! Where's your mustache?"

Danny said, "Like I said, we've got a lot to catch up on."

Blaze looked at his watch. "Alright, let's head upstairs, but I have to leave in an hour to pick up a friend."

Blaze arranged for a room upstairs for one hour and ordered a round of drinks.

"Who's your friend, Blaze?"

"Girl I met tonight at a restaurant. She's only 23 and I think in need of a little 'business time.'" Blaze put the phrase "business time" in air quotes; it was the old euphemism for sex that Victor had taught him and Danny back in the day.

"That's my boy," Victor said. "Look, Danny, this could be you, too—banging young girls. Hell, you haven't had any in over ten years! It's time to get back on the horse."

"Did I hear that right? Danny Maieye, former actor and former rock'n'roll star, has not had sex in over ten years? I refuse to believe it."

Victor offered, "You can add former priest to that list, Blazey boy."

Danny told them the story of the morning he'd hit bottom, waking up in Vegas not knowing where he was, what had happened, and who he was with; falling into the fountain, covered in vomit, hitting his head, and having a slot machine-playing nun tend to his injuries; and how, from that day forward, he turned his life around and embraced his lapsed Catholic faith.

"That's one hell of a story, Danny Boy, or should I call you Father Danny?"

"Tell him the next part, kid," Victor said.

"This afternoon I was defrocked by the Church. I am no longer a priest in the archdiocese of Los Angeles."

"Please don't tell me you were touching little boys, Danny, because that would be even weirder than seeing Victor dressed like Marilyn Monroe."

"Not our Danny," Victor said. "He was caught canoodling with the choir director, in a confessional of all places."

"Holy hell, Victor, how many times do I have to explain that she approached me and I had to push her off?"

"You can tell me a thousand times, Danny Boy, I still won't believe you."

Blaze took a sip of his cocktail. "Now that I know Danny's story, why don't you tell me why in the hell you are in drag?"

Victor recounted how his family had placed him in Shady Acres and how he tried to escape on numerous occasions only to be caught roaming the streets in the nude. "Anyway, during a moment of clarity I realized I should escape in disguise so they wouldn't find me. Since

Halloween was around the corner, I thought I could get away with dressing up as a woman as a joke for the staff. Instead of going to the party, I walked right out the door."

"And into my car," Danny offered, imitating Billy Ocean. "Victor stowed away in my car, and we've been living together ever since."

"Well I guess that's a problem solved for both of you: Danny, you have a place to stay, and Victor, you have someone to take care of you."

"Have they approached you about the show yet?" Danny asked Blaze.

"As a matter of fact, I just learned of it this evening."

"What's your take?"

"Well, to be honest, I fucking hate reality TV. It's a bunch of greedy pigs at the networks capitalizing on cheap production and a bunch of bottom-feeder wannabe celebrities without talent who appear on them. Together they are dumbing down entertainment. I think it denigrates what we do."

"I couldn't have said it better myself," Victor offered. "When I was coming up in the business you needed talent and a strong work ethic—reality TV is bullshit."

"Does that mean you're not going to consider it, Victor?" Danny asked.

"What is there to consider?" Victor replied. "They haven't even asked me yet. Besides, the minute my mug goes on TV, I'll be living back in that nursing home before you can say 'sponge bath.'"

Danny turned to Blaze and said, "Allison Hart tells me that they won't do the show unless you are on it. Are you at least considering it?"

"I was only pitched the idea tonight," Blaze said. "I've

agreed to take a meeting with this Allison Hart woman tomorrow morning. I should have more of a picture by then." Blaze paused to look at the time. "Fuck!" he exclaimed. "I have to get back to pick up Holly."

"Can we touch base tomorrow after your meeting?" Danny asked Blaze.

"Sure, what's your cell number?"

Danny gave Blaze his number, and they all hugged each other and left the club.

Blaze didn't think that the night could get any stranger, but then again, this was LA—it could always get stranger.

CHAPTER TWENTY-THREE

T-Bang Bags Blaze's Babe

It was 11:45 and Holly was waiting anxiously outside of the restaurant. Ernesto the waiter came outside to keep her company.

"Face it, sweetie," Ernesto said. "He's not coming. I've seen this happen a billion times—he's likely already found another distraction for the evening."

Holly took offense to being referred to as a distraction. "Fuck you, Ernie—when was the last time you had a date?"

"Honey girl, I am a gay man living in West Hollywood. I turn boys down left and right."

Their conversation was interrupted when a large black SUV with darkly tinted windows pulled up in front of the restaurant. Holly assumed it was Blaze and walked up to the truck; she was surprised when the back passenger-side window rolled down and she was face to face with T-Bang.

"Hey shorty," T-Bang said, "is the kitchen still cookin'? Me an' da boys needs to get some foods before heading out for the night."

Holly was in awe and couldn't even speak. Ernesto, who couldn't have cared less about the "celebrity" in his midst, said, "The kitchen closed at 11."

"That's a dirty shame," replied T-Bang. "Say, shorty, you want to go and have some fun tonight? Me and the boys are headin' to a club."

Holly replied, "Jones—yeah, I heard rumors about it on Twitter."

"Ain't no rumors, Red," T-Bang replied. "We're on our way there right now. Hop on in and hang with us; you'll be on TV."

Ernesto looked into the truck and saw what he considered to be a "who's who" of degenerates inside. For a second, he was worried that he would wind up on *Bling it On* and immediately stepped away from the vehicle. "Holly, I don't think that's such a good idea," Ernesto objected.

"Holly, such a pretty name for such a pretty girl," T-Bang said. "Come with us and we will deck the halls of da club with lots of Holly."

Holly looked at her phone again; it was now 11:50 and there was no sign of Blaze. Upset about being stood up, and annoyed by Ernesto telling her what to do, she climbed in the SUV with T-Bang and his crew. As they drove away she looked back and saw Ernesto still on the curb out front, shaking his head.

#

Blaze looked at the clock on his dashboard; it was five minutes to midnight. "Fuck!" he exclaimed. "Fuck fuck fuck!" At two minutes to midnight he pulled up in front of the restaurant, which was deserted except for one lone soul smoking a cigarette out front. As Blaze got closer he recognized the waiter who served him and Stanley earlier in the evening. Blaze pulled up to the curb and rolled down his window.

"Excuse me, Ernesto, is it?"

"Well, look who came back. Sorry, big spender, but she's gone—you just missed her."

"Fuck fuck fuck!" Blaze said again.

"You didn't expect a girl like that to wait around for a guy like you all evening, did you?"

"Do you know where she went?"

"Yes, but it is going to cost you."

"Cost me what?" Blaze asked.

"I need a ride, because I got stood up myself this evening. I'm actually supposed to go to the same place Holly was going, but I didn't want to get into the car with those thugs."

"Thugs?" Blaze asked.

"T-Bang and his boys, but judging by your age you probably don't know him."

"He's my fucking neighbor. Get in."

Ernesto got into Blaze's Porsche and Blaze sped away before Ernesto could get his seatbelt on. "What the hell?"

Blaze let up on the gas. "Sorry," he said, slowing down. "Of all the people she could go off with, it had to be him."

"Why do you care so much? You don't even know her."

"That's not the point. People go crazy over these fucking reality stars, and what have they really done to become famous? In the case of T-Bang, be born into privilege and act like a complete asshole. It's not fucking right."

"Why should you be so angry? You already had your chance at fame."

For Blaze, nothing stung more than the loss of his relevance as a celebrity, and he now was experiencing it for the second time that night. At a red light, Blaze turned to his passenger and said, "I'm Blaze fucking Hazelwood." He paused to let his proclamation, accompanied of course by his British affectation, sink in.

Sensing that he upset one of his own icons, Ernesto attempted to make Blaze feel better. "My grandmother used to let me stay up late to watch *Casa Grande*. Do you know how big a following you had in the gay community?"

"Old women and gay men, the story of my life," Blaze replied.

Letting his guard down, Ernesto went all fan boy on Blaze. "I have so many questions for you. Does Danny still look like Richard Grieco? Whatever happened to Vanessa? Is Elizabeth as much of a bitch as she seems? Do you know who stabbed your character?"

"That show went off the air 25 years ago. Tell me you've moved on since then."

"You don't get it, do you?" Ernesto replied. "That show was an escape for those of us who watched it. We wanted to be part of that show; I was crushed when it went off the air. I heard a rumor that you were on TV recently, is that true?"

"I am afraid so. Your friend T-Bang had a party one night and one of his guests broke a window in my home. I went over to confront him and wound up featured on his show."

"That must have happened when I was in Germany,"

Ernesto replied. "Plus, I couldn't care less about reality TV either. I'm trying to be an actor myself."

Blaze saw this as an opening to end the conversation about where his career had gone since *Casa Grande* went off the air and decided to engage Ernesto in conversation about himself. "Have you done anything recently?"

"Well I recently won the part of a grown-up version of Ralphie in a sequel to *A Christmas Story.* I thought it was my ticket out of the restaurant business, but production was shut down before it began as an anti-gun group raised a stink that the first film glorified guns. The studio bowed to the pressure and demanded that a key plot device, Ralphie's Red Rider BB Gun, be replaced with a harmonica. The writer refused and that was that. They even had Peter Billingsley all set to direct."

"What the fuck is the matter with this world?" Blaze muttered.

Ernesto assumed it was a rhetorical question and didn't offer a reply. "So what have you done recently?"

Blaze took a deep breath and responded, "Mostly voiceover work. I was the voice of KITT in the *Knight Rider* reboot a few years ago."

"Sorry," Ernesto replied. "It was my favorite show as a kid, but the new one didn't have the same magic. I'm sure it wasn't your fault," Ernesto offered as consolation.

"The show was doomed from the beginning," Blaze replied. "The first mistake was changing the car—to millions of fans KITT was a Pontiac Trans Am. Seeing the new Kit as a Ford Shelby was an immediate turn off. Secondly, there wasn't enough Hasselhoff in it."

"Oh, I had a thing for him back in the day."

"I am sure you did," Blaze replied and then

remembered that Ernesto mentioned being in Germany recently. Blaze wondered if this coincided with the "Don't Hassle the Hoff" festival that took place in Berlin annually in the late fall. After Oktoberfest in Munich the "Don't Hassle the Hoff" festival was Germany's biggest funfair. He then decided that he really did not want to know the answer to that question and remained silent.

They pulled up in front of the club, which had a line around the block waiting to get in. Blaze was approached by a valet and got out, tossed the valet his keys, handed him a twenty, and said, "Find me a good spot." He and Ernesto walked over to the front of the line, where he was greeted by a doorman holding an iPad.

"Name?" the doorman asked, not even looking at Blaze.

"Blaze Hazelwood."

The doorman responded, "I don't have a Hazelton on here."

"Wood. Hazelwood. And I am not on the list."

"If you're not on the list, you have to stand in line with everyone else."

"Don't you know who I am?"

"Buddy, if I had a dollar for every time I heard that line, I could retire."

Just then five women approached the bouncer, who looked them up and down. Apparently, he liked what he saw because he let them all in immediately.

"I suppose they're on the list," Blaze said sarcastically.

"Look, in order to get into this club without your name on the list you either have to be somebody or look like that. Now go to the back of the line and wait your turn." His final three words were accentuated by his pointer finger, which pushed into Blaze's breastbone three times.

While Blaze was busy with the bouncer, Ernesto was busy tweeting his experience with Blaze to the world:

Can't believe I am with Blaze Hazelwood at Jones. #casagrande
Blaze looks like he's going to punch a bouncer. #badblaze
Back of the line for us. #thisisnotgoingtobeasfunasithought

Blaze and Ernesto walked to the back of the line. Blaze stood quietly with his arms folded across his chest and his jaw clenched. "At this rate we aren't getting in until two a.m. and I've got a big meeting tomorrow."

The guy standing in front of Blaze and Ernesto looked like the spitting image of Vince Neil, the lead singer of Mötley Crüe. He turned to his friend, who bore a strong resemblance to C.C. DeVille, the lead guitarist for Poison, and said, "Oh, I've got a big important meeting tomorrow. I've got to get a manicure at 10 a.m."

Not missing a beat, "C.C." replied, "I thought you were getting a facial at 10 and a manicure at 11."

Blaze knew they were mocking him, but if there was one thing he'd learned as a child actor it was not to fuel the flames of one's critics. His restraint paid off because a few minutes later the two left the line and Blaze was that much closer to the door.

Ernesto and Blaze waited silently in line for a few minutes, until Ernesto decided to break the silence. "Is it hard being famous and losing your fame?"

Blaze was too tired to argue. "I make a better living as an actor than all of these other people standing in this line combined."

"Okay, but what I meant is, is it hard to deal with the fact that 25 years ago you would have been led right through that door and now you are in line with me and all of these other people?"

"One thing you should never take for granted is fame," Blaze said. "You want to be an actor, right?" Blaze said, and Ernesto nodded. "Well, let's say you make it and the world begins to love you. There is nothing anyone can do to prepare you for what you will experience when they don't care about you anymore. You will have people around you who will tell you what you want to hear, but usually they have some vested interest in keeping your hopes up. No one will tell you the truth; you'll just have to rely on your own coping mechanisms that hopefully you have developed over the years."

Ernesto stood there silently and took in everything that Blaze was saying. Blaze continued, "My mother had me going on auditions when I was just starting grammar school; I spent more time auditioning than I did in the classroom. At a young age I learned how to deal with rejection, and over time losing a part to another actor didn't hurt so bad. But then something happened—I started to get parts. A commercial here, a guest spot on a sitcom there, and before you know it I was acting regularly. I got *Casa Grande* when I was barely a teenager, and that show changed my life. It was a real high. But no one can prepare you for what happens when you come down."

"Hey, looks like we are almost in," Ernesto said.

Blaze had been so lost in his thoughts, he hadn't realized that he and Ernesto were now at the front of the line—or that a bunch of guys with cameras had lined up in front of the club.

"Well, if it isn't Hazleton," the bouncer said.

"Hazelwood," Blaze retorted.

131

Just then the doors of the club flew open and T-Bang, his entourage, and Holly came barreling through the doors. The cameras started clicking and the flashes started flashing.

Blaze caught Holly's eye. She walked up to him and slapped him in the face. "That's for making me wait, asshole."

T-Bang, who recognized Blaze, went up to him and said, "You just got schooled, son. This little shortly has been bitching all night about some Sting-looking dude who stood her up. That shit is crazy that it is you, bro, but check it out, she's with me, dawg."

Blaze was too stunned to reply, but when T-Bang turned his back on him, Blaze finally reached his breaking point. Not caring that he would wind up on another episode of *Bling it On*, Blaze jumped over the red cordon separating him and T-Bang and jumped on his back, knocking him to the ground. It took two members of T-Bang's entourage plus the bouncer to peel Blaze off of him. The bouncer pushed Blaze to the ground as a stunned T-Bang ducked into the SUV that the valet had pulled around, followed by Holly and the other members of T-Bang's entourage.

Blaze stood up, but his legs felt weak. He put his hand to his nose, which was sore, and when he pulled it away he saw that it was covered with blood.

The bouncer threatened, "If you are not out of my sight in ten seconds, I'm calling the cops."

Blaze didn't need to be told twice. His Porsche pulled up right then; fortunately for Blaze, Ernesto had found the valet and paid him to bring the Porsche around.

Blaze got behind the wheel and Ernesto joined him in

the passenger's seat.

"I wonder how many people saw that," Ernesto said excitedly. "Do you think you should see a doctor about your nose?"

"I just want to go home. Where can I drop you off?"

Ernesto gave Blaze his address and Blaze dropped him there, then returned to Malibu. It was after two in the morning and he wanted to get some rest before his meeting with Allison.

CHAPTER TWENTY-FOUR
Run Interrupted

Allison was finishing her morning run on the treadmill when her phone started blowing up. If there was one thing she couldn't stand it was being interrupted during her morning ritual; seven days a week and 365 days a year, Allison ran no fewer than ten miles on a treadmill. For the first half of her run she let her mind wander and thought about nothing at all; the second half of her run was her time to catch up on whatever the latest TV craze was. At the moment, Allison was binge-watching *Orange Is the New Black*. She felt a connection to the lead character, Piper Chapman. While Allison had never been involved in the drug trade or spent time in a women's prison, she shared Piper's proclivity for saying the wrong thing at the wrong time and constantly alienating those she was closest to.

So it was with a great deal of resentment that she paused the latest episode in order to answer a FaceTime call from Lucy. Within seconds Lucy's freckled face appeared on Allison's iPad.

"What do you want, Lucy?" Allison said, not panting at all; her ponytail bouncing left and right.

"Didn't you read my texts?" Lucy replied.

"What time is it, Lucy?"

"Six thirty a.m.," Lucy replied. "Why do you ask?"

"What do I always do between five and seven a.m.?" Allison asked.

"Oh, right, you're running. But listen, I think we have a problem on our hands."

"What kind of problem?"

"Have you not read the news yet this morning?"

"No news before eight, Lucy, you know my rules."

"Our boys got into an altercation last night."

"What boys?" Allison asked.

"T-Bang and Blaze had another altercation, and this time it was caught by the paparazzi. It's the front page of every tabloid and the home page of every entertainment website."

"What the hell happened?" Allison asked while still not breathing hard.

"All we could tell by the footage is that Blaze got angry at T-Bang and lost it. My favorite headline is 'T-Banged Up! Reality Star Sucker-Punched by B-Lister.'"

"Fuck, this could ruin everything! What time is my meeting with Blaze?"

"Ten a.m.," Lucy replied.

"And when is my meeting with Brandon and Catherine?"

"Eight thirty."

"Okay, so we have two hours to spin this into something positive. How quickly can you get to the office? I am going to need your help with this."

"I am already on my way."

"Excellent. I'm going to shower now and head over. I'll see you shortly."

Allison ended the video chat before Lucy could reply. "Fuck!" she screamed at the top of her lungs. "Fuck, fuck, fucking fuck."

CHAPTER TWENTY-FIVE
T-Bang Rubs it In

Blaze was awakened that morning by the sound of his home phone ringing. There was only one person who called him on his landline, and Blaze didn't want to talk to him, so he let the phone go to voicemail. It started ringing again five seconds later. Begrudgingly, he got out of bed to answer it.

"What do you want, Stanley?"

"How did you know it was me?"

"Aside from the fact that it is 2015 and every phone has caller ID, you are the only person who calls me on my landline."

"Are you trying to give me a heart attack?"

"What are you talking about?"

"Your little kerfuffle last night with T-Bang is all over the news. I wouldn't be surprised if we lose the show over this."

"Let me remind you, Stanley, that we have nothing to lose since I haven't said yes yet. As far as I am concerned, that wouldn't be any big loss."

"You know, Blaze, you can be really short-sighted. Why can't you see that this show could be the best thing to happen to you since *Casa Grande*?"

"You said the same thing about *Back to the Future: The Musical* and that didn't exactly turn out to be true, did it, Stanley?"

"This is different. Your fans want you back, can't you see that?"

"They want me so bad I have to wait in line at a club?" Blaze sat at the Mac on his desk and did a quick Google search of his name. "Jesus Christ, I'm looking through the web reports of what happened last night and half don't even spell my name correctly. The ones that do focus on T-Bang and make me sound like a crazy man."

"Blaze, I am going to give you some advice that I was given a long time ago when I was starting out in this business: If you don't like what is being said, change the chatter."

"Powerful words, Stanley, but I need a platform where people will listen to me."

"Why can't you see that you are being offered just such a platform?" Stanley pleaded.

As much as he didn't want to admit it, Blaze knew that Stanley was right. He also knew that, like it or not, *Return to Casa Grande* was the first non-voiceover part Blaze had been offered in years. He was quickly coming to the conclusion that he might have to eat crow and take the gig, but he wasn't ready to tell Stanley that.

"Are we still set to meet this Allison woman at 10?"

"It's eight and they haven't canceled yet."

"Alright, I'll meet you in the lobby at 9:45."

"Great. Can you do me a favor?"

"What's that?" Blaze asked.

"Turn on the charm that made Blaze Hazelwood a teen idol two decades ago. I get the feeling that you are going to need to pour it on thick after last night."

"Not to worry, luv," Blaze replied.

"That's the spirit, Blazey boy."

As Blaze hung up with Stanley, he heard his phone beep, indicating that he had a text. It simply said "Thank you" and was from a number he didn't recognize.

He replied:

Who is this and thank you for what?

A second later Blaze received a photo as a reply: a nude picture of Holly smiling on someone's bed.

Thank you for not picking up this shorty, and thank you for jumping on my back at the club. Highest ratings ever.

"Fuck!" Blaze screamed at the top of his lungs. And immediately received another text:

I heard that.

CHAPTER TWENTY-SIX
The Ice Queen Starts to Melt

Allison and Lucy spent an hour brainstorming; they started with the notion that any publicity is good publicity and finally landed on the following argument:

1. "Blaze Hazelwood" was once again the most-searched-for term on Google in the past 12 hours, thereby building a strong base of interest for *Return to Casa Grande*.

2. The evening's footage of the altercation between T-Bang and Blaze was the most heavily streamed footage that *Bling It On* had ever seen.

3. Controversy leads to eyeballs; there is nothing that American audiences enjoy more than conflict.

Feeling confident that she and Lucy had built a solid argument to present to Brandon and Catherine, Allison gathered her bag and walked toward Brandon's office.

"Is he in?" Allison asked Margo. She couldn't help but notice that Margo's face seemed stuck in place and her lips were twice the size they had been the day before.

Margo tried to answer, but Allison couldn't make it out.

"What was that?" Allison asked.

Margo grabbed a pad of paper and reached for a pen. She wrote, *I had some dental work done yesterday and am having a hard time talking. He's meeting with Catherine. He'll buzz me when it's time for you to go in.*

Dental work, my ass, Allison thought to herself. She took a seat in the waiting area and pulled out her phone. She was flabbergasted that she had an email from Stanley Roth waiting for her to open on her phone as she assumed he didn't know what email was. When she read the email she was equally surprised that all the words were spelled correctly; certainly Stanley couldn't type!

Allison,

I must apologize for Blaze's behavior last night. I assume we are still on for our meeting later this morning. Rest assured, Blaze will be on his best behavior from here on out.

Kind Regards,

Stanley

I hope he knows how to open an email, Allison thought as she typed out a reply assuring Stanley that the meeting had not been canceled and that she would give him an update after her meeting with Brandon and Catherine. Margo informed Allison that Brandon was ready for her.

As Allison opened the door, she saw Catherine and Brandon sitting on the couch; clearly there was more than business going on between them.

"Would you care to explain what happened last night?" Brandon asked.

"Brandon, listen, I can explain everything—"

"I don't know how you do it," Catherine said.

"Do what?" Allison asked.

"How did you orchestrate that altercation between Blaze and T-Bang?" Brandon asked. "It's all anyone is talking about. It's the perfect time to strike—we need to announce *Return to Casa Grande* immediately. Where are you with getting Blaze on board?"

Allison thought about admitting she'd had nothing to do with the fight but thought, *what they don't know won't kill them.* "Blaze is meeting with me this morning at 10 before he decides."

"Excellent," Catherine said. "Do you think it would help if I come along, to assist with your pitch?"

"I appreciate the offer, but I'd rather keep it small—he's a bit temperamental, and I don't want to overwhelm him."

"I understand," Catherine said with a hint of disappointment. "But you will be sure to set up a meeting with him and me and the Believe brand team once it's a done deal, right?"

Allison wondered what had happened to the Ice Queen. "Of course, my team is planning a launch party and we'll invite everyone on the brand team."

"Wonderful," Catherine said, blushing.

"Allison," Brandon said, "this is the biggest product launch in UPC's history. Just so we are clear, if anything goes wrong it means your job."

Allison was taken aback and couldn't hide the shock on her face. She'd doubled the Lust sales with *Bling it On Featuring T-Bang*, and now her job was on the line?

"Allison, you're in the major leagues now," Catherine

said condescendingly. "No one cares what you did last month, last week, or even last night—your future is always going to be tied up in what you are doing right now."

"I understand," Allison said coldly, thinking, *Ah, the Ice Queen has returned.*

"That's a good girl," Catherine replied.

Allison bit her tongue and just stared coolly at Catherine.

"Call me immediately after your meeting with Blaze," Brandon said. "Now, if you don't mind, Allison, Catherine and I have some important matters to discuss."

Allison thought, *if only I could prove that Brandon and Catherine were having an affair, that would mean a little job security.* But deep down inside Allison knew it wasn't job security she was in search of, she wanted power.

"I will," Allison said, getting up, shaking their hands, and leaving the office. She heard the lock on the door clicking as she walked away.

CHAPTER TWENTY-SEVEN

Meanwhile, at Denny's

While Allison was having her meeting with Brandon and Catherine, there was another important meeting going on over breakfast at a Denny's in Culver City. Elizabeth Pierce, Danny Maieye, Vanessa Crestwood, and Victor Tillmans were all seated at a round table, waiting for Stanley.

Vanessa broke the silence. "Jesus Christ, can't we order already?"

"Patience, darling," Elizabeth said. "He'll be here."

"And don't take the Lord's name in vain," Danny added.

"Fuck you, Danny," Vanessa countered. "Don't get all high and mighty on me. They threw you out of the Church anyway, why do you care?"

"Stop it, you two," Victor said sternly. He was once again dressed like Marilyn Monroe; he had yet to hear whether Allison had worked things out with the retirement home and wanted to be safe rather than sorry.

"I really need this to work out," Vanessa admitted. "I

am being evicted from my apartment and will have no place to live at the end of the month. When that woman Allison called me to discuss *Return to Casa Grande*, I thought my prayers were answered."

"Funny choice of words," Danny said sarcastically.

"Don't act like you don't need this either, Father Maieye," Vanessa said mockingly. "You can't exactly go back to hearing confessions, can you?"

"I was set up!" Danny exclaimed.

"Oh, hush, you two," Elizabeth said. "Try acting dignified for a change. You're the same spoiled brats you were 25 years ago."

"Look who's talking," Victor said. No one dared to address Elizabeth in such a manner except for Victor Tillmans. Still, Elizabeth was too stunned to respond, so Victor continued, "Don't act as if you have it all together, Elizabeth. You need this gig just as much as they do."

"How dare you!" Elizabeth said incredulously, but she stopped herself from going any further. She knew Victor was right.

Danny looked out the window and saw Stanley walking toward the front door of the restaurant. "Look, there he is now."

The hostess pointed toward the table where Elizabeth, Danny, Vanessa, and Victor were sitting, and Stanley walked over to the table and sat down.

"You wanted to see me?"

Elisabeth spoke first, "Why, Stanley, you have not aged a bit in 25 years."

"Are you fucking kidding me?" Vanessa blurted out. "He's put on at least 40 pounds and is wearing a rug!"

"I see you haven't changed a bit, Vanessa," Stanley said.

"As charming as ever." Since Blaze was the only one of them who kept working steadily after *Casa Grande*, the other stars asked Stanley to represent them as well in the hopes that he could work the same magic on them. It didn't work for any of them and they all fired him unceremoniously over the years.

"Stanley," Danny said, cutting to the chase, "what are the chances that Blaze is going to sign on?"

Stanley looked around the table and saw the faces of four very sad people. A quarter of a century ago these four people couldn't go anywhere without being asked for an autograph, and now three of them were almost homeless and the other one had to dress in drag for fear of being locked up in an old folks' home.

"Blaze and I have a meeting at 10 a.m. My sense tells me that he is leaning toward signing but has to be convinced."

"And how do you plan on convincing him, Stanley?" Vanessa asked. "It's not like he needs the money like we do, though how the hell he kept working all this time is beyond me!"

"You're right, he doesn't need the money," Stanley admitted. "But there's one thing Blaze needs more than anything else in the world right now." He let the words hang in the air for a moment.

"What's that?" Vanessa asked.

It was Elizabeth who responded, "Fame. Blaze has never adjusted to not being in the spotlight. That's what will get him back to *Casa Grande*, the promise of being relevant once again."

"Bingo," Stanley said.

"I want to address the elephant in the room," Danny

said.

"Who, Stanley?" Vanessa replied, to a burst of laughter from everyone at the table, sans Stanley of course.

Once the laughter died down Danny continued, "No, that little altercation with Blaze last night. Will that ruin our chances of this show working out?"

"Allison doesn't think it will. People are talking about the show again because of it."

"I agree," Victor offered, "but Blaze came off as a bit of an asshole."

"He is an asshole," Danny said.

"That may be true," Stanley said, "but he is our only hope for getting *Return to Casa Grande* off the ground."

"Why does he always get a pass?" Vanessa asked. "His career should have been over at least three times, yet he always manages to bounce back. I just don't get it."

Stanley said, "Vanessa, Blaze is handsome and charming; that combination goes a long way in this town."

Danny blurted out, "But he's not even a good actor!"

Everyone at the table was silent.

"You all know it's the truth! Don't you remember how many takes he needed for every scene? He couldn't take direction from anybody and could never remember his lines!"

This made Vanessa laugh. "I thought it was just me who felt that way. Remember opening night of *Back to the Future: The Musical?* The audience practically shouted out his lines for him when he couldn't remember them? It's a good thing that movie was so quotable!"

"Nevertheless," Elizabeth said, "everyone around this table needs him now, and I suggest we don't do or say anything that will ruffle his feathers."

"Always the voice of reason," Stanley said, addressing Elizabeth.

The conversation at the table was interrupted by the waitress, who asked, "What do you all want for breakfast?" The former cast members of *Casa Grande* placed their orders, as did Stanley. For the remainder of their breakfast they took a walk down Memory Lane, recalling their favorite episodes of the show that had made them famous.

CHAPTER TWENTY-EIGHT
Is this Love?

Blaze arrived at the UPC offices with a full 30 minutes to spare before his meeting with Allison. Failing to see Stanley, he decided to grab a coffee at the coffee kiosk in the lobby.

"Can I get a beverage started for you, sir?" asked a waiflike young man wearing the required green apron. His entire head was shaved except for a patch of long pink hair extending from the top of his forehead down to the bottom of his chin. Blaze looked at his name tag and saw that it read "Squeaker."

"Thank you, ahem, Squeaker. I'll take a grande blond roast."

"No problem, sir, can I have your name?"

Blaze's image was all over the morning papers and gossip sites and he was still being asked for his name. *Unbelievable*, he thought to himself. "My name is Blaze, Blaze Hazelwood."

"Oh, I just need a first name, sir," said Squeaker, who showed no sign of recognizing the name of the man

149

standing before him.

Blaze received and paid for his coffee and put the change in his pocket rather than in the tip jar. Squeaker gave him a dirty look as if to say, *would it have killed you to put your change in the jar?* Sensing this, Blaze, still stung by the barista's lack of recognizing whom he was serving, shouted, "True change comes from within, Squiggy."

"That's Squeaker, asshole."

"Squeak this, luv," Blaze said while walking back toward the security desk where Stanley was now standing and handing over his identification to the security guard.

The security guard said, "Mr. Roth, the picture on your license doesn't look like you."

"I beg your pardon," Stanley said.

"You see, in this picture you look like you are going bald. But in front of me it looks as if you have a full head of hair. Do you have any other form of identification? I am sorry to have to ask, but security is very tight here at UPC."

Security at all entertainment companies was super tight in light of threats from the North Korean government, who was upset how their country was being portrayed in American cinema and on TV. UPC was a target since a recent episode of *Bling it On* featured T-Bang and his crew doing impressions of North Korean supreme leader Kim Jong-un while high on nitrous oxide.

Seeing that Stanley was taken aback by the security guard's comment, Blaze stepped in. Reading the name on the security guard's badge, Blaze said, "Officer Gardner, I can state with all certainty that this man is Roth; Stanley Roth, that is. He doesn't look like he does in that picture because he has gained 40 pounds and acquired a hairpiece since that photo was taken."

"Is that really necessary, Blaze?" his agent asked.

The security guard nodded. "Mrs. Hart's assistant, Marios, will meet you on the 18th floor. Please affix these to your jackets; they need to be worn while you are in this building."

Once inside the elevators, Blaze removed his badge. "Do they really think anyone in this town would ruin their outfit with one of these things?"

"Blaze, listen, after the events of last night, I need you to be on your best behavior. If they say wear the security badge, wear the goddamn badge."

Blaze put the badge back on. "Happy now?"

"Quite," Stanley replied. "By the way, I couldn't help but notice that your friend Holly was involved in that little scuffle last night."

"Thanks for pouring salt on the wounds, Stanley, old boy."

"Hey, that's what I'm here for."

When the elevator door opened, a tall, thin man wearing a black suit and a skinny black tie greeted them, a headset sticking out of his left ear.

"Mr. Hazelwood and Mr. Roth, I presume," Marios said.

"That's us," Stanley said.

"My name is Marios, I'm Allison Hart's assistant, and I must say, Mr. Hazelwood, it is really an honor to meet you."

Surprised, Blaze said, "Nice to meet you as well, mate."

"*Casa Grande* meant so much to me," Marios continued. "I used to watch it with my Nana when she would babysit me. Oh, how much trouble I would be in if my parents had found out, but it was worth the risk. Come this way, I'll show you to Allison's office." Marios received a call, placed his left hand against the headset in his left ear and plugged his right ear with his index finger. "Good morning, Allison Hart's office…"

As Marios attended to his call, Blaze and Stanley followed him down the side streets and alleyways of the office floor. Marios ended the call as they arrived at the door of Allison's office suite. "Gentlemen, have a seat while I ring Ms. Hart to let her know that you are here."

Blaze and Stanley took a seat in the waiting area. There were copies of *Variety* and *Entertainment Weekly* on the coffee table and they both picked one up to thumb through.

"Oh, interesting!" Stanley exclaimed.

"What's interesting?" Blaze asked.

"Says here that Todd Bridges has signed on for a part in *Aging Ink*. I was trying to get you a part on that show, but it says here Todd was 'the last piece of the puzzle.'"

Todd Bridges had played the role of Willis Jackson on an '80s show called *Diff'rent Strokes*. Todd's struggles with drugs and alcohol were well documented, but he was the lucky one—his two co-stars were both dead.

"Todd and Danny used to party back in the day," Blaze said. "What the hell is *Aging Ink* anyway?"

Stanley turned toward Blaze. "It's actually a very clever concept. You know how kids on cartoon shows never grow up? I mean, *The Simpsons* has been on for 25 years, but Bart Simpson is still only 10."

"Right, and the kids from *South Park* should be in their 20s, but what's the point?"

"Well, someone came up with a show addressing what would happen to these animated kids if they were allowed to grow up. I mean, most child stars turn out to be complete and utter train wrecks if they live long enough to see their 30s. So this show will be taking six famous animated child stars and placing them in a reality situation as adults. The icing on the cake is that each grown-up animated child star will be voiced by a former real-life child star."

"That's actually pretty brilliant," Blaze admitted. "Who is Todd voicing?"

"Well, Todd will be voicing a grown-up Fat Albert."

Blaze interrupted, "You wanted me to voice Fat Albert?"

"No, at the time you were being considered for voicing a grown-up Brainy Smurf, but the producers had a hard time getting sign-off from Hanna-Barbera, the animation company that produced *The Smurfs*. Someone at *Aging Ink's* production company knew a guy, who knew another guy, who knew a girl that had an espresso with Bill Cosby, so they were going to pursue Fat Albert as a plan B; I guess it worked out.

"Who else is on board?" Blaze asked.

"It says here Tina Yothers from *Family Ties* will voice Penny from the *Inspector Gadget* cartoon, Corey Feldmen will voice Wily-Kit from *Thundercats*, Danny Pintauro from *Who's the Boss* will voice Elroy Jetson from *The Jetsons*, Missy Gold from *Benson* will voice Jem from *Jem and the Holograms*, and Mindy Cohn from *The Facts of Life* will voice Rainbow Brite. Dr. Drew Pinsky is set to voice the lead therapist at the house."

A well-dressed woman entered Allison's office suite and walked up to Marios's desk.

"Ms. Philips, what a nice surprise, but I don't think

Allison is expecting you now."

"Oh, I know, Marios," said Catherine, stealing a look at Blaze. "I just happened to be in the neighborhood and wanted to stop by and see if Allison has any time on her calendar later this afternoon."

"It says here that she already has a meeting with you and Brandon at four p.m. this afternoon."

"Thank you for looking into that for me, Marios. I'll leave you alone now; no need to tell Allison that I stopped by."

"You didn't notice, with your head in *Variety*," Stanley said, "but through that whole exchange that woman was looking at you most of the time."

"After last night," Blaze said, "I am not in the mood for chasing women. Plus, her perfume bothered me; it reminded me of someone from the past."

"Who?" Stanley asked.

"Throughout my time on *Casa Grande* and well after the show went off the air, I received love letters, about one a week, from a woman with the initials C.R. She always sprayed her perfume on them and it was exactly like the perfume that woman was wearing."

"Oh, the horror," Stanley said sarcastically.

The phone on Marios's desk buzzed and he answered, "Yes, okay, I'll show them in now." Marios turned his attention to Blaze and Stanley. "Allison is ready for you now." Marios opened the door to his boss's office and ushered Blaze and Stanley inside.

"Thank you, Marios," Allison said. "Gentlemen, will you please have a seat?"

Blaze was half expecting Allison to be just another boring corporate executive; he was surprised to see a stunning woman in her late twenties or early thirties come around her desk to shake his hand.

"Mr. Hazelwood, is everything okay?" Allison asked, as he held on to her hand. Blaze just kept staring at her blindly.

"Oh, no," Stanley said. He knew what that look meant; he was love-struck. "Ms. Hart, you'll have to excuse Blaze here, he had a bit of a rough night last night and I'm not sure if he is fully recovered." Stanley then did the only thing he knew to do: punched Blaze in the arm. "Are you with us, Blaze?"

"Wait, what?" Blaze replied and then remembered where he was. "Sorry, I guess I am a little stunad from the events of last night." Blaze used the Italian word for "stupid"; while his mother's family was Jewish, his father's family was 100 percent Italian and stunad was one of his favorite words.

"Funny," Allison said, "my father used that word all the time, whenever I seemed spacey."

"Have we ever met before?" Blaze asked. "I feel as if I know you from somewhere."

This made Stanley nervous; he was familiar with all of Blaze's pickup lines and this was one of his classic go-tos.

"I can assure you, Mr. Hazelwood," Allison began to say.

"Blaze, call me Blaze."

"I can assure you, Blaze, that this is the first time we've met."

"Why don't we get down to the business of why we are all here," Stanley said. "*Return to Casa Grande*."

"Good idea," Allison said. "Blaze, I know you have some reservations about the show, which is why I'm glad we can meet and discuss this personally. Blaze, can you hear me?"

Blaze was staring at a picture on Allison's office wall. "What is that doing on your wall?" he asked, pointing at a picture of Allison and T-Bang.

"That was taken at an event for our Lust brand. The brand sponsors T-Bang's show *Bling It On*; I actually created that show, which actually is one of the reasons we are here. When you made an appearance on the birthday party episode, we saw the reaction you got from the public and saw an opportunity to build a show around you."

"That guy," Blaze said, referring to T-Bang, "represents everything I find distasteful with entertainment today. What is he famous for? Running around Hollywood and acting imbecilic?" Normally Blaze wouldn't lose his cool in the presence of a beautiful woman, nor would he dare to jeopardize his chance to land a part on a show, but his disdain for reality TV was so great Blaze found himself throwing caution to the wind.

"Calm down, Blazey boy," Stanley said. "Remember, we are here to see how we can make *Return to Casa Grande* work for you, not analyze the entire genre."

"I understand the points you are making, Blaze," Allison said calmly. She was well aware of Blaze's reservations, as Stanley had shared them with her previously. She was prepared with her response. "The funny thing is, I don't disagree with anything you are saying; I agree that celebrities should have to earn their celebrity, just like you had to. However, I am also a businesswoman, and it's just a fact that people like T-Bang grab attention, and attention helps to move product. The Lust brand went from being a $200 million brand to a half-a-billion-dollar brand, and our market research suggests that this was because of *Bling It On*."

Acknowledging Blaze's point of view had appeared to work. He was listening, so she continued.

"Whether you like it or not, Blaze, the brands that sponsor television shows want to see a positive return on their marketing investments, and that is exactly what they are getting with shows like *Bling It On*."

"But people will think I am desperate if I resort to reality television!" Blaze protested.

"Blaze," Allison said calmly, looking into his eyes, "I truly believe that the world wants to know what has been going on with you and your former co-stars over the past two and a half decades. There is a lot of nostalgia for the 1980s right now, and your showing up on *Bling It On* helped to ignite that. I think the story will be 'Blaze Hazelwood returns' and not 'Blaze Hazelwood sells out.'"

"Allison," Stanley said, "why don't you tell Blaze a little more about your vision for the show?"

"Great idea, Stanley. Most reality TV today is either contest-based, like *Survivor* or *The Apprentice*, or it is voyeuristic, like *Keeping up with the Kardashians*."

"*Or Bling It On*," Blaze interrupted.

"Yes, or Bling It On," Allison agreed. "But that is not what we are interested in doing with *Return to Casa Grande*. We actually want to create a new reality format for this show—a hybrid of the two." Allison paused, partly for dramatic effect and partly to ensure that she held Blaze's attention. Seeing that he looked interested, Allison continued, "We want to put you and your co-stars back into the Malibu mansion where the original show was shot and have you re-create some of the classic scenes from the original show."

"But where does the reality angle come into play?" Blaze asked.

"In two places," Allison said. "Throughout filming, you and your co-stars will live in the mansion where the exteriors for the show were filmed, and all the interactions you have with each other will be recorded; these interactions will be edited and will make up half of each episode. The other half will be you and your co-stars acting out scenes from a prior episode. But you won't know what episode you will be asked to re-create until one hour before shooting, giving you and the rest of the cast only sixty minutes to prepare."

"Tell him about the viewer involvement aspect," Stanley said.

"Since our market research tells us that the reality shows that do best are those with viewer involvement," Allison said, "the episodes you will be asked to re-create will be decided by the viewers. Furthermore, viewers will vote on which cast member did the best job during each reenactment. The cast member with the most votes at the end of the season will become the new spokesperson for a Universal Products Company brand and earn a paycheck of one million dollars."

Allison and Stanley stared at Blaze, awaiting his reaction.

"So there is an acting component to this after all," Blaze said.

"Yes, definitely," Allison said reassuringly. "You and your castmates will have to act your socks off—aside from there being one million dollars on the line, the winner's face will be everywhere: on TV, billboards in high-exposure places like Times Square, print advertisements, and the Internet. Fame can be yours once again."

Allison knew this last bit was risky, as it implied that Blaze was no longer famous; but she also knew it was what he wanted most, the most tempting carrot she could dangle in front of him.

"Is the one million dollars the only compensation, or is there a per-episode fee?" asked Blaze.

Allison looked at Stanley, who replied, "For each episode you appear on you will earn $50,000 in a combination of cash and UPC stock."

"How does that compare to what the rest of the cast is getting?"

"It's about twice the amount any of your co-stars would receive, but let's keep that between us, shall we?"

Allison continued, "We are also working out a deal with the original writers to write a final episode of *Casa Grande* that would air at the end of the season. The idea is to answer the question that has been on every fan's mind since 1989: Who stabbed Kyle Dixon?"

Allison saw Blaze's face light up at this news, so she decided it was time to go in for the kill. "Blaze, I only have one question for you: do we have a deal?"

Both Allison and Stanley looked intently at Blaze, who placed his hands on either side of his mouth, as if he was saying a silent prayer to himself; Blaze knew something about drama and decided to hold the others in suspense for a minute.

Finally he responded, "Yes, I believe we do."

CHAPTER TWENTY-NINE
The Melting Continues

It was just before noon, and Catherine Philips had been staring at her office phone for the better part of twenty minutes. She wasn't typically the anxious type, but seeing Blaze in person had made her nervousness skyrocket. "It's been at least 20 minutes since that meeting ended," she said out loud, in an uncharacteristically whiny voice. "Why hasn't anyone called me yet?"

Catherine prided herself on maintaining a stoic appearance, but this was getting to be too much. She was reaching for the phone when it began to ring, and she almost jumped out of her chair. A quick glance at the caller ID told her it was Brandon calling. Normally her executive assistant, Alan, would pick up the phone, but he was under strict orders not to answer when Brandon was calling.

"Brandon, darling, tell me you have some good news for me."

"I just got off the phone with Allison and..." Brandon paused for dramatic effect.

"Don't fuck with me, Brandon. Is he in or out?"

"In, baby. Blaze Hazelwood is all in."

Catherine sat back in her chair and allowed a smile to form on her face. She took a deep breath and remained silent.

"Catherine, are you still there?" Brandon asked.

"Oh, I'm here alright, but not for long."

"Where are you going?"

"Have Margo clear your calendar between 12 and two, and send her out for an extended lunch. We have some celebrating to do."

CHAPTER THIRTY

Phonebooth Nightmares

Stanley left the UPC offices a very happy man. That morning he hadn't been sure Blaze would buy Allison's pitch, but her including a competitive element to the show was nothing short of genius. Giving Blaze the chance to act on TV versus being the subject of a purely voyeuristic reality show was the proverbial icing on the cake; Blaze had admitted as much before they parted company in the lobby of the building. Stanley glanced at his watch—he needed to call Elizabeth Pierce as soon as he could find a pay phone.

Stanley had to walk seven blocks before he found a phone, which was currently in use by a homeless person, who was not actually using the phone to place a call, but as a urinal. "All yours, buddy," the homeless man said in a raspy voice while exiting the phone booth. "Don't forget to flush," he cackled as he walked down the street pushing a shopping cart full of his possessions.

He was mortified at the prospect of entering the phone booth, but he was even more scared at Elizabeth's wrath if he was late in calling her. After all these years and even after her fall from grace, Stanley was still scared to death of Elizabeth Pierce.

Stanley reached into his tight-fitting pants and struggled to pull a few quarters out of his pocket. He picked up the receiver, slid a quarter into the slot, and dialed Elizabeth's number. She picked up on the third ring.

"Elizabeth Pierce," she said.

"Elizabeth," Stanley said panting, "it's me, Stanley."

"Stanley, you sound absolutely dreadful. Have you been running?"

"I had to walk a ways to find a phone. I have good news for you, though: Blaze is in!"

"Oh, I am delighted to hear that, Stanley. Delighted indeed. Tell me, when do we start seeing the money?"

"I'll be working out the final contracts with the UPC executives this afternoon. But they've agreed to pay each actor a signing bonus up front. After that, you will each get an appearance fee to participate in some promotional activities, and from there on out you'll each get paid per episode."

"And what about the living arrangements?"

"UPC has offered you one of their corporate apartments to use before you move back into the *Casa Grande* mansion. It's yours as soon as you sign the contract."

"I have to say, Stanley, I didn't think you had it in you. I'm impressed."

Compliments were not something Elizabeth Pierce dealt all that often, so Stanley took her backhanded compliment as a small victory. "Are we square then?" Elizabeth had long known a secret about Stanley that would ruin his career if it ever came out; from the beginning of her career, she had learned that in Hollywood secrets were more valuable than cash.

"Stanley, my dear, you have my word that your secret will be safe with me. For now." And then all Stanley heard was a dial tone.

Stanley turned around in order to exit the phone booth. He was dismayed that his foot was sticking to the floor and had to use more force than should have been necessary to lift it up. He actually broke a sweat as his left foot came out of his shoe. His excess weight prevented him from bending down to pick up his shoe without planting his foot in the puddle of urine that had pooled on the floor. *I am way too old for this shit,* he thought to himself.

CHAPTER THIRTY-ONE

The Cupcam

Joe Jeffries ran the security and surveillance division of the Universal Products Company. His office was in the same building as Allison's, but it may as well have been across town: the different division heads knew where their departments stood, priority-wise, based on how close, or in Joe's case, how far away, they were from the CEO's office.

Joe was sitting at his desk tinkering with a prototype when Allison Hart knocked on his door. "Are you Joe Jeffries?" she asked.

Joe put the prototype down on his desk and replied, "Guilty as charged."

"I'm Allison Hart, from Entertainment; nice to meet you." She looked around his spare office, which had no window. "Joe, I'll get down to business. We've put together a new reality show, and we're hoping we can use some of your new cameras to help capture high-quality footage. The thing is, we need them to be really inconspicuous."

"How inconspicuous?" Joe asked, with a hint of

excitement in his voice; he always welcomed a challenge.

"We'll be filming the show in an old Malibu mansion. We'll have a professional camera crew on hand to capture much of what goes on, but I want to be sure we don't miss the real juicy stuff that happens after our cameras are off."

"I have something in the works that sounds perfect for what you need." Joe took out a tablet computer and placed it in front of Allison, then pulled up an app that launched a list of files. He clicked on a file, and Allison watched her entire conversation with Joe play back on the tablet's small screen.

"The video quality is amazing and the sound is, too."

"Full HD," Joe said proudly.

"Based on the angle of the recording," Allison said, "the camera must be somewhere on your desk. But all I see is a bunch of paper and a Starbucks cup."

Joe picked up the Starbucks cup. "Let me introduce the Cupcam. One of our engineers was inspired by the nanny cam and challenged himself to build something much less conspicuous that could be used in police operations. The camera is so tiny, it could be hidden anywhere; and instead of being hardwired into a digital video recorder, it broadcasts its signal over a Wi-Fi connection. So long as a recording device is on the same Wi-Fi network as the camera, it will work flawlessly."

"So how am I able to view it on this tablet?"

"That's the beauty of the Wi-Fi solution. Right now both the Cupcam and the tablet are on the UPC wireless network. Because the tablet has a playback feature, the recording device uses the tablet as its DVR. You could also use the app to watch whatever the camera sees live in real time."

Allison felt her heart rate start to speed up with excitement. "The Starbucks cup makes sense, because people are always walking around with them, and they won't look out of place if left around the set. Could these micro cameras be put into any other package? Say a bottle of body wash or a stick of deodorant?" Allison was thinking how perfect it would be if the products that would launch with Project Fountain actually held the cameras that were recording the show.

"I don't see why not," Joe said. "There's one more feature I'd like to show you. Tap the transcription button over there."

Allison did what she was told and immediately saw a perfect transcription of their entire conversation. "Amazing," she proclaimed, impressed.

"The security industry had faced a problem for a long time. Security systems will record 24 hours of footage, most of which goes unwatched unless there is a problem. But how do you know there's a problem if you're not looking for one?"

"Okay," Allison said. "Where does the transcription come into play?"

"Let's say you go on vacation and your house is wired with this technology. You come home and don't see anything missing, so you don't think to look at your security camera footage. But most thieves make at least some noise when they break into a house; some will even have conversations with a partner. So we developed this system, whereby you can select a time frame and see if any sounds were made. The system will flag anomalies and you can go right to that time in the video and see what was going on in your home at that time."

"Interesting," Allison said.

"There's one more feature in here that you may find interesting. We've built in a sentiment analysis function so that you can tell the mood people are in based on the language and tone they are using. We did this specifically for a government agency who wanted to reduce the number of man hours spent on stakeouts. Instead they wanted to plant bugs in a person of interest's home or office and use our software to more efficiently identify incriminating conversations."

"Is that legal?" Allison asked.

"Ask Uncle Sam," Joe retorted. "He paid for it."

"I'm thinking this could be very useful for the show," Allison replied. "We're going to have hundreds of hours of footage to sift through every week and can only use a fraction of that for the show. This will reduce editing time significantly!"

"Glad to be of service," Joe replied.

Allison thought about her meetings with Brandon and Catherine. "Joe, how many of these Cupcams do you have right now?"

"Three, including the one you're holding in your hand. Why do you ask?"

"Could I borrow this, just until the end of the week? I want to show it to Brandon Master when I meet with him in, shit, twenty minutes!"

"I'll let you borrow it on one condition," Joe said.

"What's that?" Allison asked.

"That you put in a good word for me and the division with Brandon. I know he's close with Brian Philips, and my little division could use all the internal PR we can get."

"Show me how it works," Allison said, "and I will

happily sing your praises."

Joe downloaded the Cupcam app onto Allison's smartphone and showed her how to livestream and play back the footage, as well as use the text analytics tools. Allison then picked up the Cupcam and started the long trek back to Brandon Master's office.

CHAPTER THIRTY-TWO

Blaze Starts Obsessing

It was three o'clock in the afternoon, and Blaze was obsessing. Ever since he'd set eyes on Allison Hart he could not get her out of his head. There was something about her that was familiar, but he couldn't put his finger on it. He needed to see her again but knew it would be inappropriate to ask her on a date; he needed a business reason to see her. For that, he needed Stanley. He held down the home button on his iPhone and said, "Hey Siri, call Stanley Roth."

"Okay, calling David Lee Roth," Siri replied.

Blaze hit the end call button. "No, Siri, call S-T-A-N-L-E-Y-R-O-T-H," he said, slower this time."

"Checking the web for articles on Hyman Roth. Here's what I found…"

Blaze pressed the home button on his phone forcefully, but then realized his mistake. "Siri, call My Fat Agent."

"Okay," his phone replied, "Calling My Fat Agent."

The phone rang four times and then Blaze shouted, "Oh bloody hell, Stanley, answer your phone!"

After the fifth ring, Blaze heard the click of Stanley's answering machine come on. "You've reached the office of Stanley Roth. Your call is very important to me, so please leave your name, number, a brief message, and the time of your call and I will return your call shortly."

"Stanley, it's Blaze Hazelwood calling. You know my phone number and the time of day is approximately half past your asshole. Call my cell phone as soon as you get this message. I'm heading out to a six p.m. focus group, but call me anyway."

Blaze then hopped in the shower as the first step in his transformation into a stay-at-home father named Jimmy. After his meeting at UPC, Blaze answered a call from Mary at the focus group facility in Westwood, asking if he could pass as a stay-at-home father for a focus group on baby accessories targeted to dads. The clients wanted a mix of both working and stay-at-home fathers, and the facility was a little light on the latter. Blaze said yes, more motivated than ever to build his acting chops.

Blaze took the elevator to the 11th floor and checked in with Mary at reception.

"What study are you here for?" Mary asked.

"Mary, it's me, Blaze," he whispered. "Don't you recognize me?"

Mary put her hand to her mouth and whispered back, "Wow! This is your best disguise yet. I love the fake teeth and the wig. You look like a different person. Have a seat over there with the other dads, your group will begin shortly."

Blaze took a seat in the waiting area and looked around at the other guys, thinking to himself that he had never seen a sadder-looking group of guys in his life. It was close to six p.m., but four of them were wearing sweatpants and the other three were wearing what Blaze termed "dad jeans." To Blaze, a group of stay-at-home dads wreaked of desperation and dejection; he thought to himself, *I may be voicing a clay figurine with a ball gag and a boner, but at least I am not as sorry as these guys.* He took his phone out of his pocket to see if Stanley had called. Nada.

"They are going to make you turn that off, you know," said one of the dads to his right. His nametag said "Bill."

"Pardon me?" Blaze asked.

"Your phone—they always ask you to turn them off in the group. They get kind of anal about it, worse than an airline."

"I can't wait to turn mine off," chimed in another participant named Chris. "It'll be the only two hours of peace I get all day."

"Last night I was giving my kid a bath," chimed in a third dad named Nick, "and my wife texted me to find out what I had planned for dinner. I was like, if only you knew the day I had you wouldn't be asking me."

"So what was for dinner?" Blaze asked as a way of getting into character.

"Chicken piccata," said Nick, deadpan, at which all of the men in the waiting room, including Blaze, erupted into laughter.

"I see you're all getting to know each other out here," said a fortyish male wearing jeans and an untucked shirt. He seemed way too happy to be one of the participants. "I'm Mike and I will be your moderator this evening. We're just about ready to begin. All I ask is that you all turn off your cell phones before entering the room."

Blaze had already decided he would not comply, as he

was going to take Stanley's call come hell or high water.

"How about you there, partner—can you turn off your phone for me?"

"Actually, I can't," Blaze replied.

Mike looked down at Blaze's name tag. "And why is that, Jimmy?"

"Because my kid is home alone and I need to be available in case he needs me."

Mike took a minute to look up "Jimmy's" profile information on the respondent summary he held in his hand. "It says here, Jimmy, that you have one child aged five. Are you telling me that you left a five-year-old home alone?"

By now, the eyes of all the fathers in the room were on Blaze. "What I meant to say," Blaze said, "is that this is the first time I am leaving my son with a sitter, and I want to make sure he can get a hold of me if he needs to."

"Okay," Mike said, sounding unconvinced, "but if it becomes a problem I am going to have to ask you to leave and you will not receive your incentive payment. Is that clear?"

"Quite," Blaze said.

They all entered the room and Blaze chose a seat next to the door, in case he had to get up and take a call from Stanley.

Mike the moderator then began going over the ground rules for the session, letting all the participants know that the session was being recorded and that there were observers watching from behind the mirror located behind him.

"Now, let's spend some time getting to know each other. Please take a moment to introduce yourself, including your name, the number of children you have, their ages, and something you like to do for fun. Bill, let's start with you."

"Hi everyone, my name is Bill and I have two kids: Mark, who is eight, and his little sister Mary, who will be four and a half tomorrow. Acknowledging the half birthdays is important! For fun I enjoy participating in triathlons and playing poker with the guys."

Next it was Chris's turn to introduce himself. "Hi, my name is Chris, but everyone calls me Sonny." Mike the moderator made a note of this. "I have a seven-year-old son named Echo, and for fun I play drums in a Dokken tribute band on the weekends."

"Ah, Dokken was a favorite of mine back in the day," Mike the moderator said. "When's your next gig?"

"This Saturday we're playing at Mr. Scary's in West Hollywood. The name of our band is Under Lock and Key. Come check us out."

Next up was Nick. "Hi, my name is Nick and I live in West Hollywood with my partner, who is in the film industry. We have a 12-month-old daughter named Bella and she is the light of our lives. When I am not spending time with her I spend my time doing yoga or Pilates."

"I tried Pilates once. Once!" Mike the moderator joked.

"My name is Fabio and I am the father of a newborn named Miles. I am a freelance writer and the primary caretaker of my son. Oh, and I live in Silver Lake."

"Have you written anything we may have seen recently?" Mike the moderator asked.

"Have any of you heard about my blog, Hipster Dad? It was recently mentioned on the Huffington Post after I did a post on how to dress your baby like a hipster." Fabio looked around the room; no one showed any sign of recognizing his blog. "Well, you can all check it out at hipsterdad.com."

It was now Cameron's turn to introduce himself. "My name is Cameron and I have three-year-old twin girls, Jeanie and Sloane. When I am not spending time with them you can find me auditioning for commercials or taking acting classes."

"We have something in common," Mike the moderator said. "You have twins and I have triplets—two girls and a boy, and they just turned 13."

Mike's admission was met with a bunch of oohs and aahs from all the other dads in the room, all except Blaze, who kept staring at the phone in front of him. Normally he would be "in character," but Blaze was too preoccupied with the fact that Stanley had not returned his call that he stopped paying attention to what was happening in the focus group room.

"Happy to see you survived that long," Cameron said. "That tells me that there is hope."

"It gets easier as they grow up and become more independent," Mike reassured Cameron. "Jimmy, last but not least," Mike the moderator said, motioning toward Blaze.

Blaze, fixated on his phone, did not recognize the name Jimmy.

"Jimmy, you are up," Mike the moderator said impatiently.

Blaze looked up and found everyone was staring at him. "Sorry," Blaze said apologetically. "My name is Jimmy and I live in Woodland Hills. I'm a carpenter by trade, but the economy has been tough as of late, so I decided to stay home with my son while my wife went back to work." Blaze enjoyed making up the backstories for his focus group characters. He gave them occupations that he would have considered if he weren't an actor; other past occupations included fireman, policeman, and airline pilot.

"We know that your son is five from our conversation outside," Mike said, "but what is his name."

"His name?" Blaze hadn't given any thought to what his son's name was. Just then he saw his phone start to vibrate on the table; the caller ID told Blaze that it was his agent calling. "Stanley!" Blaze said out loud, annoyed. "I am sorry, everyone, but I have to take this call...it is my son calling. Stanley."

"Take it outside," Mike the moderator said disdainfully.

Blaze stepped outside of the room and answered his phone. "Stanley, you fat fuck!" He didn't realize how loud he was talking, nor that everyone in the interview room could hear him. "Why the hell haven't you called me sooner? I've been waiting all fucking afternoon."

"Sorry, Blaze, but I've been busy negotiating your contract as well as the contracts for the other cast members of *Return to Casa Grande*. Now tell me, what is so important?"

"She's the most beautiful woman I've ever seen," Blaze said, his voice still loud in his excitement. "I've been with thousands of women in my life and you would think that one corporate executive wouldn't make the needle move, but she's different."

Inside the focus group room Nick whispered to Chris, "That's an odd way to talk to a five-year-old."

Chris said, "This is LA, man, anything goes."

"Blaze," Stanley pleaded, "I don't think it's a good idea to mix business and pleasure, particularly with your love 'em and leave 'em track record."

"Let me make this clear, you wig-wearing overweight prick: give me a reason to meet with her tonight or I don't do the show."

Stanley sighed and picked the lesser of two evils. "Tell her you have a few ideas for the show that you want to talk to her about."

"Thank you, Stanley, my boy," Blaze said much more calmly. "Now was that all that difficult?"

"Just don't fuck this up for us, Blaze," Stanley said. "There's a lot riding on the success of this show."

"No worries, mate," Blaze said with his British affectation. "I'll talk to you later."

Blaze ended the call and want back into the interview room, where he found the other five participants and Mike the moderator staring at him. "Where was I? Oh, my child's name is Stanley and on the weekends I like to ——"

Before he could finish his sentence Mike the moderator interrupted him. "Are you really a stay-at-home dad, or are you faking it just to earn the incentive?"

"How dare you accuse me of lying!" Blaze responded with mock outrage.

"Prove that you have a son named Stanley," Mike demanded. "Show us at least one picture."

"I don't walk around carrying pictures of Stanley with me," Blaze protested. "Who does that?"

At that point the other focus group participants took out their phones, turned them on, and started sharing pictures of their kids with one another.

"Surely you must have a picture of Stanley on your phone," Mike the moderator said, not letting up.

Blaze knew he was caught but decided to thumb through the pictures on his phone anyway. Most of the pictures on his phone were selfies of himself or pictures of his various sexual conquests. He came to the photos of Natalie. There was Natalie in her bra and panties. Then Natalie in just her panties. Then no panties. Then Natalie on her knees, from behind, etc. Blaze got distracted and forgot what he was doing.

"What's the matter, Jimmy?" Mike the moderator said. "No pictures of Stanley on your phone?"

Blaze knew he was beaten and removed his wig and his fake teeth. "Should I leave now?" he asked.

"Don't let the door hit you on the way out," Mike countered. "I'll make sure you never get called for another focus group in this town!"

"Who gives a shit?" Blaze countered while storming out of the room. "I'm Blaze fucking Hazelwood!"

Fabio turned to Nick and said, "Blaze Hazelwho?" to which Nick replied, "Exactly."

CHAPTER THIRTY-THREE

Blaze gets a Date

It was 6:30 and Allison Hart was lying on the couch in her office reflecting on the second meeting she'd had that day with Brandon and Catherine. She'd thought they would be excited that Blaze was on board, but instead they'd just grilled her about the communications plan for announcing the show. She'd explained the plan's three primary components: an interview with the cast on the network's morning news program, a weeklong media tour for the cast on satellite radio and daytime talk shows, and a live event covering the move-in day. Kitty Carson of *The Soapdish* was lined up to cover each event. This latter part was huge news; Kitty Carson remained a household name for the millions of women who followed soap operas, and her publication *The Soapdish* remained one of the most widely circulated weekly magazines in the country. Having both on board gave both credibility and reach to her program.

Ever since Blaze had signed on that morning, Allison and her team had been hard at work getting everything lined up so they could hit the ground running. She wasn't expecting Brandon and Catherine to kiss her feet, but she also wasn't expecting them to grill her as hard as they had. In fact, right before the meeting came to an end, Catherine had threatened that if the show brought any bad press to the Believe brand it would mean Allison's job. Allison assured them that everything was under control and that they had nothing to worry about. Before leaving the room, however, Allison left the Cupcam on Brandon's desk; as long as no one moved it, it had a direct view to the couch in his office. If he and Catherine were having an affair, the Cupcam was sure to catch it.

While lying on the couch in her office Allison stewed while thinking about the other ways in which Catherine had berated her in recent weeks. She was asked to buy Catherine lunch as if she was some kind of low-level assistant who hadn't gone to Harvard, a fact she shared with the cafeteria's cashier. There was the time when she was asked to attend a Believe brand team meeting and was introduced by Catherine to her team as Amanda Hunt instead of Allison Hart. She just about reached her boiling point when Catherine asked her to stay late for an eight p.m. meeting and wound up canceling at 7:55.

The phone on her desk began to ring. Marios had left for the day, so she had to answer it herself; she cleared her throat and then picked up the receiver.

"Hi, this is Allison Hart."

Her voice was met with silence on the other end of the line.

"Is anyone there?" She glanced at the caller ID and noticed an 805 number; whoever was calling lived north of LA. "Hello!" she said forcefully.

Blaze Hazelwood had never suffered from shyness with a woman before, but at that moment he was absolutely tongue-tied.

"I'm hanging up now," Allison announced.

"Wait, don't hang up. Allison, it's me, Blaze."

"Hazelwood?" Allison asked, confused. "Is everything okay? Why are you calling me? Don't tell me you're having second thoughts."

"No, sorry, nothing like that. I am just a bit frazzled, that's all." Blaze pulled himself together, remembering what Stanley has suggested. "Listen, I was wondering if you might be interested in meeting for a drink or for dinner tonight. My schedule cleared up and I have some thoughts about the show that I would like to share with you."

Allison found it a bit strange that Blaze was calling her out of the blue, but she had to admit that after the afternoon she'd had a drink sounded really good. "You know what, why not? Did you have a place in mind?"

"Whereabouts do you live?"

"Manhattan Beach."

"Alright," Blaze said, "there's a great wine bar there called—"

"Crazy Grapes," Allison said. "I know it well. They have great small plates, too, if we feel the need to nibble on something."

Blaze was happy that she liked the place, but all he could think of nibbling on was Allison. "What time would be good for you?" he asked.

"If I leave here now, I could probably get there in an hour. Why don't we meet there at eight?"

"Eight. Great. It's a date," Blaze said happily.

"Not a date," Allison said. "A business meeting."

"Of course," Blaze assured her. "See you then."

Allison hung up the phone wondering what she was getting herself into. Then she remembered some advice her mother had given her a few years back. "Live a little, Allison—life's too short not to have a little excitement in it." Allison contemplated taking her laptop home with her but decided against it. "One night without work won't kill me," she said to herself.

CHAPTER THIRTY-FOUR

Allison gets Ammunition

Blaze estimated he had just enough time to hit the gym and shower before making the trek down to Manhattan Beach to meet up with Allison. *This is crazy*, he thought to himself. *I've never felt this way about a woman before. Is this what love feels like?*

He showered and changed clothes in record time and was back behind the wheel of his Porsche before the engine had a chance to cool down. He arrived at the restaurant at five minutes to eight and had the valet park his car. Inside the restaurant, he glanced at the bar but didn't see Allison waiting for him.

"Are you meeting someone here?" the hostess asked.

"Yes, she's about 5'5" with blonde hair and blue eyes and is the most beautiful woman I have ever seen."

"So she looks just like you but shorter?" the hostess asked, flirting openly with Blaze.

Just then the door to the restaurant opened and Allison walked in.

"That must be her," the hostess said. "Wow, she actually

does look like you. Are you two related or something?"

Blaze knew there was something familiar about Allison, but he didn't think it was related to her looks. He just felt instinctively that he knew her.

"Can we get a table away from the door?" Allison asked. "This November weather is a bit chilly for me." The current temperature was a chilling 67 degrees, which by LA standards was considered grounds for a fire in the fireplace and a heavy sweater.

The hostess showed them to a table in the bar area toward the back of the restaurant. "Is this okay for you?"

"Yes," Blaze and Allison said at the same time.

"Jordan will be your server tonight and he will be right over."

"Thank you," said Allison and Blaze, again at the same time.

Blaze pulled out Allison's chair for her, and they sat down. "So tell me, how was the rest of your day?" Blaze asked.

This question took Allison by surprise. Most of the men she met in LA were so self-involved that they rarely took the time to ask her a question, let alone pretend to listen to her answer.

"Well, to tell you the truth my day was a bit of a roller coaster. It started off with the news of your altercation with T-Bang—there are no hard feelings there, by the way. He actually laughed about it when I talked to him."

"Thanks," Blaze said, reddening. "Pure stupidity on my part."

Allison continued, "Then we had our meeting, and the day got better because you agreed to the show. I also had a meeting with a guy from our security department, who showed me some cool technology that we are going to use in the show and that was actually quite fascinating."

"What kind of technology?" Blaze asked.

Allison gave him an overview of the Cupcam, to which he replied, "That's James Bond kind of stuff. Okay, so what happened after your meeting with the tech guy?"

"After that I had a meeting with Brandon Master, who runs the entire company, and Catherine Philips, who oversees the entire Believe brand. They beat me up a bit."

"Is that the same Catherine who was in your office earlier when Stanley and I were waiting?"

"What did she look like?" Blaze described Catherine to a tee. "That's her, but Marios didn't tell me she stopped by. Strange."

"Well, after your day it's no wonder you took me up on my offer to buy you a drink."

Their conversation was interrupted by their server, Jordan. "Have we had a chance to decide what to drink tonight? Perhaps an appy or two?"

"Do you have a sauvignon blanc from New Zealand?" Allison asked.

"Why yes," Jordan said and then pointed to it on the menu. "The Kim Crawford is excellent, as are the Oyster Bay and the Nobilo."

"I'll have the Nobilo," Allison replied.

"And for you, sir?"

"I'd like a full-bodied cab, what do you recommend?"

"If it were me I'd go with the Silver Oak from the Alexander Valley. It's a personal fave."

"Sounds good to me," Blaze said.

"Can I place an order for any small plates while we wait for your wine?"

"Not yet," Allison said. "Check back when our glasses are empty and we may place an order."

"Sounds good," Jordan said and was off to the bar to get their wine.

"So you heard about my day," Allison said. "Tell me about yours. What did the mighty Blaze Hazelwood do after leaving our offices?"

Obviously, Blaze did not want to tell her that he spent the entire afternoon obsessing over her, so he made up a quick story about the day's events. "Let's see, I left your office and had lunch in Beverly Hills with an old friend of mine at a lovely restaurant called Angelini Osteria, and then went home to review my lines for an upcoming voiceover project."

"Can I ask what you are reading for?"

Blaze told her that he accepted offer to voice the part of Christian Clay in *Fifty Shades of Clay* and explained that it was a claymation spoof.

"That sounds hysterical," Allison said. "So what did you do after that?"

Blaze felt so comfortable with her, he decided to let her in on his little secret. "I actually participated in a focus group."

"My stars, why would you do such a thing?" Is money that tight? My college roommate and I used to do them to make some extra money while in school, but I can't imagine why anyone like you would need to do a focus group."

Blaze was taken aback by Allison's use of the phrase "my stars"; it was something he remembered his father saying frequently when he was growing up. Blaze explained that he used focus groups as a way of playing different parts and practicing his craft. "I try to make the others believe that I'm a plumber, or a doctor, or whatever it is I am supposed to be; it's actually helped me fine-tune my craft quite a bit."

"That's pretty brilliant," Allison admitted. "I never thought about it that way."

Their conversation was interrupted when Jordan arrived with their wine. "Is there anything else I can get for you two?" he asked after placing their wine glasses on the table.

"Not just yet," Allison replied, then focusing her attention back on Blaze she raised her glass and said, "Here's to *Return to Casa Grande.*"

"To *Casa Grande,*" Blaze replied, raising his glass. He found the courage to wink at her before taking a sip of his wine.

"So tell me, where did Blaze Hazelwood grow up? I must say, I did some snooping on you, but what I found on IMDB and Wikipedia seemed like it was written by a publicist."

"Remind me to fire her," Blaze joked. "I was actually born in a small town in New York State called Little Falls."

"Sounds quaint," Allison said.

"It's practically right out of a Hallmark movie," Blaze replied.

"You would know," Allison quipped back, referring to Blaze's history of doing Hallmark Hall of Fame movies.

"You have done your homework on me! Anyway, it was the kind of town anyone with ambition couldn't wait to leave, and my mother felt the same way. She moved me to California when I was five and I went on audition after audition. I did a few commercials here and there and some one-off appearances on some popular shows, but *Casa Grande* was my big break."

"Just you and your mom went to California?" Allison asked. "What about your father?"

"Dad was the sole heir to a family farm," Blaze replied. "He wanted nothing to do with California and refused to come with us, that's what my mother said anyway. My mother told me he was having an affair and was going to leave her anyway; she figured it was better to be a single mom in Los Angeles than a single mom in Little Falls."

"That must have been hard on you," Allison said sympathetically.

"It was even harder after my mother died when I was 18. I've never felt so alone in my life. But I had money because of *Casa Grande*, so I was able to take care of myself. I was a spoiled 18-year-old orphan."

"Did your father ever try to contact you? Surely he must have known that his son was on one of the hottest TV shows."

"He did, once. He managed to track down my home address and sent me a Christmas card, with a photo of him and his new wife and their daughter. He aged well, but I didn't want anything to do with him. The way I see it, he didn't care enough about me and my mother to keep the family together, so why should I look to have any relationship with him?"

"Wow, you've gone most of your life without speaking to your father. I don't know what I would do without my dad—he's my rock."

"Tell me about him," Blaze said.

"Well, parts of him remain a mystery," Allison started.

"He was older when I was born, so he was more mellow than most of my friends' dads. Although I must admit at times I was embarrassed because when my friends met him for the first time, they assumed he was my grandfather."

"Was your mom younger?"

"She was fifteen years his junior," Allison said. "They met one summer on vacation in Massachusetts, in a bar; the way they tell it, it was love at first sight."

I wonder if history is repeating itself, Blaze questioned.

"They were married for 25 years before we lost my mother to cancer."

"I am very sorry to hear that," Blaze said. He noticed that their wine glasses were just about empty. "What do you say we get a refill on these and then place an order for some tapas? All this talk has worked up my appetite."

"Sounds good."

Over more wine and food, Blaze and Allison talked about anything and everything, like two long-lost friends. Blaze was amazed by how easy it was to talk to Allison and how natural it felt to be in her presence.

When they were finished, Blaze offered to pay the tab, but Allison insisted that they split it fifty-fifty. Blaze knew better than to argue with her; he could tell she was used to getting what she wanted, and that was part of what made her so attractive.

"I know it's cold out tonight," Allison said, "but how would you feel about taking a walk on the beach with me? I find that putting my feet in the sand and water is a great way to end the day."

"Sounds like a plan to me," Blaze said happily.

They walked the few blocks down to the beach and

removed their shoes. "Race you to the water," Allison said, and started toward the water with a head start.

"No fair," Blaze protested, and ran after her. He caught up with her quickly and they declared the race to be a tie.

As they walked, Allison said, "When I was little my parents would take me to the shore and I would play on the beach all day, even after the sun went down. It was part of the reason I wanted to come to California after graduating from Harvard."

"I didn't even see the ocean until my mother moved me out here. Now I can't imagine living away from it."

They started walking down the shoreline, when Allison took Blaze's hand and placed it in her own. This caused Blaze's heart to beat a little faster. "Is Hazelwood your real last name?"

"Hazelwood is no more my real last name than Blaze is my real first name," Blaze replied. "I haven't told anyone my real name in over 30 years. Partly because I'm not that person anymore and partly because I haven't felt close enough to anyone to open up about it."

"I know what you mean," Allison said. "When I came to California I took my mother's maiden name as my last name because I wanted a fresh start."

Blaze wanted to be respectful of Allison's privacy; she didn't push him to share his name, so he didn't push her to share hers.

"It's getting kind of late," Blaze said. "Why don't we start heading back? I'm sure you have a busy day tomorrow. Come on, I'll walk you to your car."

"I like this side of you, Blaze Hazelwood. I thought you were just another spoiled LA actor, but it turns out you're kind of sweet."

They were still holding hands when Blaze decided to pull her close. Their bodies pressed against each other, they stared into each other's eyes. Blaze felt as if he was holding the most beautiful woman he had ever held, but he couldn't help but feel that whatever was happening between them was more than just attraction—he felt a sense of familiarity with her. The moon was full and they could see each other clearly and Blaze waited for a sign that it was okay to kiss her, but she never provided one; instead they maintained eye contact for an awkward minute like two inexperienced teenagers. Allison broke eye contact first.

"I definitely feel a connection with you, but I want to take it slow. We are going to be working together and I don't want anything to jeopardize the show."

"I understand," Blaze said, with a hint of disappointment. "What do you say we call it a night and end on a high note?"

"Sounds good, Mr. Hazelwood," Allison said.

#

When Allison got home, she decided to take a bath before going to bed; her feet were sandy from their walk. Plus, Blaze had managed to get her all worked up, and taking a bath was one way Allison had learned to cool her jets.

After her bath, Allison grabbed her phone to see if anything had transpired in Brandon's office after she left. She found the Cupcam app on her tablet and opened it. Instead of jumping directly to the video, she decided to start with the transcript view.

After she'd left, Brandon and Catherine spoke at length about the launch plan for Project Fountain. Catherine presented some market research that suggested they could bring up their sales projections. Then things got interesting.

Speaker 1 (female): "That's not all I want to bring up."

Speaker 2 (male): "I don't think I can manage to do it again."

The software didn't know who was speaking but was smart enough to assign different designations to each speaker based on the pitch of their voices. At this point Allison decided to switch to video view, to place this part of their conversation in better context; or at least that's what she told herself.

Switching to video view, Allison saw that Catherine had straddled Brandon. Her bare back was pointed directly at the Cupcam.

"That's not the answer I was looking for!" Catherine said, taking Brandon's hands and placing them on her ass.

"I still haven't recovered from our lunch meeting," Brandon said wearily.

"You're missing a word in your excuse, slave," Catherine said angrily, reaching between Brandon's legs and giving him a not-so-gentle squeeze.

"Madam. I still haven't recovered from our lunch meeting, madam," Brandon said.

"That's better, slave," Catherine said, loosening her grip on Brandon's manhood.

Catherine then stood up, turned around, and faced the camera, her back to Brandon. She hiked up her skirt to reveal her panties to Brandon and demanded he remove them. When Brandon started taking them off she forcefully said, "Not with your hand, slave. With your mouth."

Brandon did what he was told. At that point Allison

decided that she had seen enough. She slept easily that night because she knew that she had leverage on the one person who was making her life difficult. And then there's the fact that she had put her Vibratoe to good use.

CHAPTER THIRTY-FIVE

Crossing the T's

Allison and Lucy were busy putting together all of the pieces of the *Return to Casa Grande* communications plan. Since UPC was a national TV network, they landed a coveted segment on the morning news show *Morning Roast*. The two anchors from the show were going to fly out to LA and conduct an interview with the cast on site at the Malibu mansion where *Return to Casa Grande* was going to take place. In addition, on a segment producer's recommendation, Allison and T-Bang were going to be interviewed about trends in reality TV prior to the cast interview; Allison was careful to hide this news from Blaze for fear that he would lose his mind sharing a stage with T-Bang.

In the two weeks since Allison's dinner with Blaze, she hadn't seen him much; he was busy recording his voiceovers for *Fifty Shades of Clay*, and she was busy with the launch. But he had sent her flowers every single day, creating rumors that she was having a fling with Blaze. To say that Catherine Philips was jealous over these rumors was putting it mildly; she had scheduled several last-minute meetings and created plenty of other curveballs designed to frazzle Allison, but throughout it all she'd maintained her composure.

"Marios, are we all set for the *Morning Roast* event?" Allison asked her assistant.

"Everything is set," Marios said. "We have limos scheduled to pick up you, T-Bang, and the Casa Grande cast at 3:30 a.m. so that you get to the mansion no later than four in time for hair and makeup. You segment goes on right at 4:30 a.m."

"That is such an ungodly hour!"

"Everything is done this way so it airs live in NY at 7:30 in the morning. I am told that is when viewership peaks."

"How did everything go with Shady Acres?" Allison asked.

"Fine," Marios replied. "They were very appreciative that we called to let them know Victor was safe, as they had been unable to get anyone in his family to return their calls. Danny Maieye has been granted power of attorney over Victor's affairs; Shady Acres wanted to be clear of any liability should anything happen to Victor."

Allison had had a chance to meet him and the rest of the cast over the past two weeks and saw nothing wrong with Victor. "I wonder why he was in a place like that anyway," she said. "He seems to have it together, except for the whole Marilyn Monroe thing."

"That's the one thing I liked about him," Marios joked.

"Well, fortunately he doesn't need that disguise any longer."

"Am I wrong to be feeling really good about where we are with this?"

"You've worked like an animal these past few weeks, Allison, you should feel great about it."

"Well, I still have to go to Malibu this afternoon to check in on the set," Allison replied. The exteriors for the original show were shot at a mansion in Malibu that actually had a vineyard on its property. It had been listed for sale at a price that was high even for Malibu standards, so Allison had made an offer to rent it for one year at an astronomically high rental rate. The offer was accepted. Allison wanted to check on the site since it would be where the network interview was taking place the day after tomorrow.

"Would you like me to get you dinner reservations at Mastros?" Marios asked, referring to Allison's favorite restaurant on the water.

"That's a good idea. Why don't you make it for two, at seven p.m." Allison had already made plans to see Blaze that evening, since he lived very close to the set.

"No, Marios," a voice said, "make it for three, at 7:30." The voice belonged to Catherine, who had come into Allison's office uninvited and unannounced.

"Catherine, what a pleasant surprise," Allison said, masking her frustration. "To what do I owe the pleasure?"

"I understand that you are going to be visiting the set," Catherine said coolly. "I would like to see it as well and make sure that everything is on brand." The Believe team was extremely uptight about its brand and had dictated a long list of dos and don'ts, for everything from the angle of product placement to the color of the walls inside the set.

"I can assure you that everything will be as you requested," Allison said.

"You know what they say," Catherine countered. "Seeing is believing. Say, doesn't Blaze live up that way?"

Allison was curious why Catherine was so interested in Blaze. She was married to the CEO of the company and was having an affair with the company's president—what could she possibly want with Blaze Hazelwood? "Yes, as a matter of fact, he does live in Malibu. Why do you ask?"

"Well, maybe he would like to meet us on set. You could arrange that, couldn't you, Allison? I hear you two are pretty close."

Feeling stuck, Allison said, "I'm sure if he has time he would love to join us."

"Excellent," Catherine said. "Marios, why don't you give Blaze a call and set it all up. Text my assistant the address, I'll have my driver take me over." With that, the Ice Queen was off and Allison let out an audible sigh.

"At least you don't have to drive with her," Marios said.

Allison had packed a bag in the event that Blaze invited her back to his place this evening, and now she felt disappointed; that would be unlikely with Catherine joining them for dinner. She felt a special connection to Blaze that she didn't really understand. She had only been with him a few times, yet it seemed whenever they talked they could finish each other's sentences; she had started predicting when he was going to call and what kind of mood he would be in when he did. *It might be love*, she thought to herself.

CHAPTER THIRTY-SIX

Allison gets Trumped

"Don't bite your lip, Anaclaysia, you know what it does to me when you bite your lip!" Blaze said into a microphone.

"That was better, Blaze," the voice director called out into the studio. "Now give me half a beat between the first time you say 'lip' and when you say 'Anaclaysia.'"

Blaze hated voice directors; he was now on the fifteenth take for this line. It was the last one he had to record for the day, and all he wanted was to go home and then meet Allison at the set. He relented and delivered the line as told.

"Great," the director said. "That's a wrap, folks."

Blaze said his goodbyes and made a beeline for his Porsche. It was four o'clock and he had to make it from Burbank to Malibu by six p.m. He was dying to see Allison.

#

Allison had gotten stuck in some traffic on the drive out, but now that the Pacific Ocean was on her left, she felt like she was in heaven. Despite her reservations about Catherine's joining them, she was dying to see Blaze.

She passed Mastro's Ocean Club on the left-hand side and her stomach began to growl; she realized she had skipped lunch again. Allison forgot to eat when she was engrossed with work.

As she passed Pepperdine University on the right, she knew she was getting close. Just then she saw a white limousine in her rearview mirror come riding up fast behind her; she swerved into the right lane for fear that she would be rear-ended. The windows of the limo were tinted, so she couldn't see inside the car, but she did get a glimpse at the license plate: it said BELIEVE. "Fucking bitch!" she screamed at the top of her lungs.

She sped up, attempting to catch up to the limo, which was several cars ahead of her now. Unfortunately for Allison, the police officer on a motorcycle parked around the bend didn't care that she was trying to catch up with Catherine and immediately put on his flashing lights after she flew by. The limo driving Catherine hit its brakes after seeing the cop and slowed down long enough for Catherine to roll her window down, stick her hand out the back window, and wave goodbye to Allison.

"Bitch!" Allison screamed again.

CHAPTER THIRTY-SEVEN
Blaze Gets a Personal Tour

Blaze arrived at the mansion at ten past six and was surprised that the only other automobiles in the driveway belonged to the crew, who were working inside; he'd expected to see Allison's BMW.

The mansion sat atop a large hill; from where Blaze was standing, he saw a white stretch limo pulling into the driveway. He watched as it slithered its way up the curvy driveway and pulled alongside Blaze's Porsche; he watched as a tall and slender woman in her late 40s got out. Blaze recognized Catherine Philips right away, from the smell of her perfume.

"You must be Blaze Hazelwood! I can't tell you how excited I am to finally meet you!" Catherine said excitedly. "My name is Catherine Ros—" She caught herself almost accidently giving her maiden name instead of her married name. "Philips. Catherine Philips, and I run the Believe brand for UPC."

"Yes, I believe I saw you in Allison's office the other day, looking to schedule a meeting or something."

"We have no doubt that this show will provide a very successful launch of our new product line," Catherine said. "We are all very excited about it."

Blaze thought it was odd that Catherine kept staring at him with what seemed like a silly expression on her face. "It will be good to relive some of the *Casa Grande* magic, as well as help you sell some more soap," Blaze said jovially.

"Oh, we don't call it soap," Catherine said. "Believe is comprised of moisturizing agents and gentle cleansers. It is important that you never refer to it as soap." She linked arms with Blaze and began walking him toward the front door of the mansion.

"Have you heard from Allison?" Blaze asked. "I thought she would get here before me; I'm surprised that I beat her here."

"She called me earlier and told me that she was caught in an unexpected meeting with Larry Wilcox, of our colleagues, and that I should go ahead and give you a quick tour. Tell me, how long has it been since you have been to this set?"

As Blaze walked towards the mansion, arm in arm with Catherine, he couldn't help thinking that women in southern California tended to be a bit more aggressive and forward than women from other parts of the country; even for a successful senior executive at a world-class corporation, Catherine's behavior was strange.

Blaze responded, "Actually, the only things filmed here were the exterior shots of the vineyard and the home; everything else was filmed on a soundstage in Culver City. So I've actually never been in the mansion itself."

"Well, then, by all means, let me give you a tour."

Blaze and Catherine walked in through the front door

into an impressive entryway: There were two staircases approximately 15 feet from the door that met at the top, almost in a heart-shaped pattern, and to the right of the front door was a dining area that was bigger than most LA apartments. To the left was a gigantic living room that had not one but two fireplaces in it. One walked through that room to get to the kitchen, which, with its white cabinetry, hardwood floors, and top-of-the line stainless steel appliances, could have been featured in *Architectural Digest*. On one side of the kitchen was a three-season room with a full bar and fireplace, while on the other side of the kitchen was a study designed with dark mahogany wood and rich leather couches.

"Wait until you see the upstairs," Catherine said. The truth was, it would be her first time seeing the upstairs, since this was actually the first time she was setting foot in the house.

"I think I better wait down here for Allison," Blaze protested. "She told me she wanted to be the one to show me the house."

"What's the matter, Blaze? I don't bite," Catherine joked.

"Fine, take me upstairs," Blaze said. "I'm all yours."

CHAPTER THIRTY-EIGHT

Speeding Gets You Nowhere, Fast

Officer Joseph Getraer of the Malibu police department got off of his motorcycle and walked to the passenger side of Allison's car. Once Allison saw him approaching her passenger side she rolled down the window and smiled at the officer, hoping that being pretty polite could get her out of a ticket.

"Do you know why I pulled you over, ma'am?" Officer Getraer asked. He leaned his head through the window partly to hear her response and partly to smell whether or not there was any alcohol on her breath; he found that many women in Malibu tended to enjoy cocktails during the day, and he had a lot of collars for DUIs in the early evening.

"I may have been exceeding the speed limit somewhat, Officer," Allison replied. She tried to sound shamed but feared that she may have come across as insincere, which, of course, she was.

"You were going 80 in a 55! Why were you in such a rush?"

Allison couldn't explain that she was trying to beat a cold-hearted bitch she referred to as the Ice Queen to a TV set, so she just pleaded ignorance, "Honestly I wasn't aware of how fast I was going, Officer."

"Give me your license and registration please. I'll run it and bring it right back to you."

Allison handed the officer her license and registration and watched him go back to his motorcycle through her rearview mirror. Allison thought that with modern technology it should not take that long to look up one's driving record and to check the registration, but for some reason cops always took their time with doing so. Fortunately for her she did not have any accidents or speeding tickets in the past five years and thought that maybe she would get off with just a warning.

Ten minutes later Allison saw Officer Getraer get off his bike and approach her vehicle, once again from the passenger side. "Well, Ms. Hart, aside from a number of tickets for jaywalking, you have a very clean record, but I am going to have to give you a ticket; under normal circumstances I'd let you off with a written warning, but the city of Malibu is running at a budget deficit and your contribution to counteract that problem will be about four hundred dollars. You can contest it if you want, but I recommend you do the right thing and just pay the ticket."

Officer Getraer then handed Allison back her license and registration as well as the ticket for four hundred dollars. Allison placed the registration back into her glove compartment, her license back in her wallet, and the ticket on the passenger seat of the car. "Have a good day, ma'am, and please drive more slowly."

Allison rolled up the passenger side window, turned on her left blinker signaling her intention to pull back into traffic and made her way towards the mansion. She estimated that she lost about twenty minutes of time as a result of being pulled over, and there is no telling what Catherine was capable of doing in twenty minutes. She feared the worst!

CHAPTER THIRTY-NINE

The Ice Queen has a Meltdown

Upstairs in the mansion, Blaze and Catherine ran into some painters who were putting away their supplies. "Excellent," Catherine said.

"What's excellent?" asked Blaze.

"This color is so on brand!" Catherine exclaimed, standing in one of the bedrooms.

Blaze was getting impatient. He'd come to spend some time with Allison and instead found himself stuck on a guided tour with a narcissistic executive.

"You know, I was a big fan of Casa Grande back in the day," Catherine said. "I was crushed when it went off the air."

"Is that so?" Blaze said. He was starting to feel uncomfortable; since the painters had left, Blaze and Catherine were alone upstairs.

"Oh, yes," she said, almost purring. She put her arm around him, faux-casually dropping her hand below his waist.

The old Blaze would have accepted Catherine's

advances without hesitation, but the new Blaze, the Blaze who was falling in love with Allison Hart, didn't want anything to do with it. He tried to pull away, but Catherine had a surprisingly tight grip. "What's the matter, Mr. Hazelwood, you don't like older women?"

When it came to women and age, Blaze didn't discriminate. In his younger years especially he was infatuated with older women, sometimes much older women, as he felt they could teach him a thing or two about performing in the bedroom. He only had one major regret when it came to his cocksmanship, but that was a long time ago and he doubted that anyone but him even remembered.

In addition to Catherine's advances, another thing was troubling Blaze: her perfume. All of a sudden, something clicked. "Earlier, when you introduced yourself, you started to say something and then cut yourself off."

"I don't know what you are talking about," Catherine protested, attempting to move her hand from the back of his waist to the front.

"You said Catherine Ros...and then stopped. What was your maiden name?"

"Why would you care about such a thing?" Catherine groaned. "We are two consenting adults in this great big house, let's do the things adults do in such situations." Catherine then took her hand, which was now just below Blaze's stomach, and brought it downward. "Oh, my, it's bigger than I imagined it would be, and I have imagined this for so long."

Blaze swatted Catherine's hand away forcefully, which made her crazy with Lust. "I love a man who plays hard to get."

"C.R." Blaze muttered. "Were your initials C.R.? Were you the one that wrote me all those letters?"

"You remembered!" Catherine said. "I can't believe you remembered! Oh, Blaze, we are destined to be together forever!"

Neither Blaze nor Catherine had noticed Allison standing in the doorway. From what she saw, it was clear that Blaze had no interest in Catherine, but she wanted to see how strong his will actually was.

"What letters?" Allison said. Blaze and Catherine both turned toward the doorway. "And why is your hand on my boyfriend's cock?"

"Allison, so nice of you to join us. I see you are wearing a new suit—did a new shipment come in to the thrift shop?"

"Boyfriend?" Blaze said.

"Yes, boyfriend," Allison said. Blaze took a giant step back from Catherine. "What is all this about letters?"

"Back in the '80s, when Casa Grande was at its peak and years after it went off the air, I received a lot of fan mail. Over time the amount dwindled, but one person always wrote to me, once a week, up until the mid-'90s. She doused each letter with a particular perfume and signed each letter with the initials C.R."

"Catherine Rosdale," Allison said.

Catherine looked at Blaze intently. "We are soul mates," she said. "When you showed up on Allison's little show, I took it as a sign that fate was bringing us together. Can't you feel it, Blaze?"

"Well, Catherine, it looks like I have something that you want," Allison said, walking toward Blaze. They hadn't kissed yet, but nothing would have made Allison happier than seeing the expression on Catherine's face as she kissed Blaze right in front of her. Standing in front of Blaze, she put her hands around his head and kissed him on the mouth. It was an intense kiss, fueled by both passion and the desire to make another woman jealous, and oh, how it worked!

"No, no no, no, no!" Catherine protested. "I've dreamed about this moment since I was 15 years old. Blaze and I would kiss, then I would lead him to the bedroom, where I would act out all my wildest fantasies on him and he would love me forever, and we would have babies, and..."

"Like my father always told me," Allison said, "you can't always get what you want."

"Weird," Blaze said. "My father used to say the same thing to me all the time."

Catherine started walking in circles in the middle of the room; she was pulling at her hair with both hands and repeating, over and over again, "No, no, no, no, no. He loves me. No, no, no, no, no, he loves me." It was almost as if she no longer realized Blaze and Allison were still in the room. She appeared to be laughing and crying at the same time.

"I think we better get her driver to take her home," Blaze said. "Do you want to do that, or should I?"

"I think you better go. I don't trust her up here alone with you."

Catherine began muttering, "Smart girl. Smart girl. Smart girl," sounding more like a parrot than a corporate executive.

"I don't want you alone with her either. Why don't we both go and send the driver up?" Blaze said.

"Yes. Both go. Yes. Both go," Catherine said.

Allison and Blaze walked down the stairs and out to the driveway. They knocked on the limo driver's window and explained that Catherine seemed to be having a nervous breakdown and he should call an ambulance.

The ambulance arrived within five minutes. The paramedics jumped out of their truck and introduced themselves as John Gage and Roy Desoto. The former had long dark hair worn in a style popular in the late 1970s, while the latter had thinning hair but long sideburns from the same era.

"We received a call about a woman having a nervous breakdown," Roy said. "Where can we find her?"

"Second floor, back bedroom," Blaze said.

Johnny and Roy took out their kit and ran inside.

Blaze said, "Three hours ago I was reciting smut into a microphone, and at the time I thought that the day couldn't get any weirder. I was wrong."

"Are you still up for dinner?"

There was nothing Blaze wanted more than to have dinner, and hopefully dessert, with Allison. However, the phone in his pocket started vibrating. It was Stanley. "I am sorry, but I have to take this," Blaze said.

Allison heard Blaze spew a string of obscenities into the phone and then hang up.

"What was that all about?" Allison asked.

"I need to go back to the recording studio and re-record some lines for Fifty Shades of Clay. Apparently, the recording engineer did something to today's recordings and they need to be redone. Can I take a raincheck on dinner?"

"Of course," Allison said, but not without hinting at her

disappointment. "I'll just go home and play with my toe."

"Pardon me?" Blaze asked.

"Never mind," replied Allison. "I'll see you tomorrow."

CHAPTER FORTY

Don Carboni Misses his Son

Donald Carboni was a widower two times over. Although his first wife, Annie, left him, they were never technically divorced, so he became a widower when she died of a heart attack in 1987. He had one son by her, Robert, or Bobby as he was known as a kid, whom he had not spoken with since the day Annie kidnapped him when he was five years old. His second wife bore him a daughter, 15 years after the birth of his son, but died of cancer ten years ago.

In the early days of his first marriage, the couple had longed for a child, but for whatever reason he and Annie could not conceive. As a result, they turned to what was then considered a highly experimental and controversial approach to conception: in vitro fertilization, or IVF, whereby some of Annie's eggs were extracted from her ovaries and infused with some of Don's sperm. A few of the resulting embryos were then implanted back into Annie, while the remainder were cryogenically frozen. And that is how Robert came into this world. His conception came at a steep price; Don had to sell part of the family farm to fund it.

Not a day went by that Don didn't miss his son; on his birthday every year he baked a cake, and would even light candles, but Bobby never came home to blow them out. He could never forgive Annie for the way she'd left him— with a note saying she didn't want to live the life of a farmer's wife any longer and she was going to take their son to Hollywood to try and capitalize on his good looks in the movie business. On false premises, Annie managed to get a restraining order against her husband, thus preventing him from making contact with her or their son; it damn near broke Don's heart.

Don's second wife, Carolyn, was the love of his life. Although he always swore he would never get married again, that all changed when he met her while vacationing in Massachusetts after selling his family farm. He sold the farm out of practicality; the Carboni family line ended with him, as he had no brothers, sisters, or offspring to pass the farm on to. He felt it was time to leave the hamlet of Little Falls, so he sold all of his family's land, including the farmhouse that was built on it, and headed off to see the world.

He and Carolyn were married within six months of meeting each other. At first her family objected, due to the large age difference between the two, about 15 years. Don was closer in age to Carolyn's father than he was to Carolyn, but over time they came to love and accept him. They tried for a while to have kids, but tests would show that Carolyn was infertile; she was born without ovaries, so not even IVF was an option. Don told her that he and his first wife still had some frozen embryos at a fertility clinic. Carolyn agreed to have some of those embryos implanted in her, and nine months later she gave birth to their daughter, Allison Carboni.

If Don had one wish, it would be that he and his two children could be together just once before he left this world. It was a wish Don feared would never come true.

Initially Don was upset that Allison decided to use her mother's maiden name in the professional world, but he had to admit that Allison Hart sounded more professional than Allison Carboni. After Allison's mother died, Don moved from their Connecticut home to New York City, as city life was something he had always wanted to experience; and that's where he was when he received an unexpected phone call from his daughter. Although Don and Allison were very close, they had not spoken for a month, largely because she had been busy at work. He knew she was a marketing executive who did something in television, but he really couldn't say what it was.

"Hey, darling," Don said into the phone. "To what do I owe the pleasure?"

"I know it's been a while, Dad, but I have been very busy with work. You wouldn't believe the day I had!" Allison proceeded to tell her father about her burgeoning love interest and how his choosing her over another woman had sent the other woman to the hospital.

"Sounds like my first wife," Don said. "I can't wait to see you this week, thank you for flying me up—I'm on a fixed income now."

Her father had plenty of money but never missed a chance to drop his fixed-income line on Allison.

"Hey, I have a surprise for you, I am going to be interviewed on *Morning Roast* and got you a pass to come and watch the interview."

"My stars, isn't that exciting. I can't wait to see my little girl in action."

"Also, the guy I was telling you about before is going to be there, and I would love for you to meet him."

"I wouldn't miss that for the world."

"Thanks, Dad. I'll see you tomorrow night."

"See you then, baby doll." Even though his daughter was a grown woman, he still called her by the nickname he'd given her when she was a little girl.

CHAPTER FORTY-ONE

The Morning's Roast

Morning Roast was the most-watched morning news program in the country. The show's success rested in the chemistry between male co-host Cody Sullivan and female co-host Cricket Montgomery—surprising, as the two had gone through a nasty and very public divorce years earlier. Today, the two were thousands of miles away from their New York studio and were sitting inside the mansion where *Return to Casa Grande* was going to take place.

While the show took its news elements very seriously, the producers also knew that viewers didn't want to be hit over the head with heavy news as they were waking up, so they built in pop culture segments as well. Cody Sullivan was looking into the camera and practicing his introduction of Allison Hart and T-Bang. In his earpiece, Cody heard the producer say, "We are live in three, two, one." This was his signal to start talking.

"Today we are pleased to have with us two people who are changing the game when it comes to reality television. Allison Hart and T-Bang, welcome to the program."

"It's good to be here, Cody," Allison replied.

"True dat, dawg," T-Bang said.

The two could not have looked more different. Allison was dressed in a slate-gray business suit, expertly tailored to show off her curves, and a long Coachella scarf; more than once, she caught Cody staring at her legs in her high-heeled boots. T-Bang, on the other hand, was wearing jeans that were four sizes too big for him, a flat-brimmed baseball cap worn sideways, and giant gold chains worn outside of his fur coat.

"Allison, I want to start with you. You have an MBA with a concentration in marketing from Harvard—how did you wind up creating reality TV?"

"I've always had a passion for marketing, Cody. When I was at Harvard I looked around at what my friends were watching and noticed two things: one, they didn't watch much scripted television at all, and two, they didn't watch programs when they were broadcast, they watched them at their own time, on their own terms."

"A phenomenon known as time-shifting," Cody said.

"Exactly," Allison agreed. "During my final year I wrote a business case arguing that in order to receive maximum exposure for their products, consumer goods companies should no longer rely on advertising, but instead find ways to get their products showcased in programming. In addition to that, the programming should be unscripted so that it is more real and in line with emerging consumer tastes as well as be available on demand on any platform, be it TV, tablet, phone, or computer."

"I guess this is a good segue to you, T-Bang; your show, *Bling It On*, is the first show that Allison created. Data from a recent survey of 18-to-24-year-olds suggests that more of them are aware of who you are than they are aware of the current pope, the vice president of the United States, or Ronald McDonald. Sales data made public by UPC shows that since your show has been broadcast, sales of the Lust brand have more than doubled—in fact, retailers are struggling to keep it on the shelves. We've even heard reports that some school systems across the country are banning the use of Lust in school, because teachers are complaining about scent clouds that follow young men back into the classroom after gym class. What do you think of all of this?"

"The kids want to smell like T-Bang, who could blame 'em?"

This comment was met with laughter from everyone on the set.

"To what do you attribute the success of the show?" Cody asked.

"Well," T-Bang said, "it's like this: I lead an interesting life, a life that many people covet but will never have for themselves, so the next best thing is to watch me do my thang day in and day out."

"Our market research shows it's an escape for most people," Allison confirmed.

"I am told we only have time for one more question before the end of our segment," Cody said, placing a finger against the earpiece in his ear to better hear the question being piped in from the director in the control room. "What's next for you, Allison?"

"We have a very exciting announcement to make about our next project, which will bring back five of your favorite soap stars from the 1980s, living under one roof."

"Where can our viewers go to learn more?"

"Well, Cody," Allison said confidently, staring into the camera, "if your viewers stick with UBN through the commercial break, they'll hear all about it."

Inside the studio a camera panned across the stars of *Casa Grande*, while Cody provided a voiceover: "Do you recognize anyone here? Find out more in two minutes."

Allison's father was on the patio of the mansion as the network requested that all non-essential personnel watch from a monitor outside. As he saw the camera pan over the cast of *Casa Grande*, he became increasingly uncomfortable.

CHAPTER FORTY-TWO
Tensions Run High

Tensions were running high in the makeshift green room, where the stars of *Casa Grande* were waiting to be taken to the makeshift set. Blaze Hazelwood was seeing red. "Why didn't anyone tell me that T-Bag was going to be here?" Blaze yelled at Lucy Nichols.

"Probably because we were afraid you would act like this," Lucy answered. "And his name is T-Bang!"

"I don't understand why that no-talent ghetto wannabe gets so much attention. What has he done to deserve it?"

"He's interesting," Vanessa offered. "I think he's kind of cute."

"Oh, please, little girl," Elizabeth snapped. "You'd sleep with anything that moves."

"Spend any time with your buddy Johnny Walker this morning, Libby?" Vanessa retorted, using a nickname she knew Elizabeth hated.

Elizabeth had indeed started drinking when she first woke up and was still sneaking sips out of a flask whenever she could get away with it.

Danny felt it was his responsibility to play peacemaker. "Alright, settle down everybody. We are all a bit punchy. Let's all take a deep breath and be thankful that we have the opportunity to be on this show together this morning."

"Put a cork in it, Father Maieye," Elizabeth shouted.

Just then, Allison strode into the room. "What the hell is going on in here? I could hear you guys arguing all the way from the set."

"He started it." Vanessa pointed at Blaze. "He has some jealousy issues over your friend T-Bag."

"Bang," Allison corrected Vanessa. "Listen, I need you all to be on your best behavior. We are about to announce to the world that the cast of one of the most beloved prime-time dramas ever is going to reunite for the first time in 25 years! We need to build excitement for the show. The whole segment won't be longer than five minutes, can you all behave for that long? Save the fireworks for the show!"

"Two minutes to show time," a young producer wearing a headset announced.

Allison needed this to go well. She looked at her phone and saw she had two text messages: one from Brandon and the other from Catherine. Brandon's text simply read "Nice job with the segment. Keep up the good work." Catherine's, on the other hand, was less supportive: "Don't fuck it up. I am watching you. I am closer than you think."

With one minute to show time, a production assistant came in to the green room, escorted the cast to the set, positioned them where each was supposed to sit or stand.

CHAPTER FORTY-THREE
Stranger than Fiction

"Welcome back," Cricket Montgomery said into the TV camera directly in front of her. "Have you ever wondered what happened to some of your favorite nighttime drama stars of the '80s? Our special correspondent Kitty Carson is here to shed some light on the stars of the genre's hottest program, *Casa Grande.*"

The studio monitor showed a photo montage of the cast from the '80s, followed by some clips of the show's most memorable moments. Kitty Carson provided the voiceover: "It's hard to believe that it's been 25 years since we said goodbye to *Casa Grande*, a show that to this day is held up as the gold standard of prime-time drama. Back then the cast members—including Elizabeth Pierce, Vanessa Crestwood, Danny Maieye, Victor Tillmans, and breakout star Blaze Hazelwood—could not go anywhere without being mobbed by fans and paparazzi. However, Hollywood has a short memory, and the show was largely forgotten—that is until recently, when Blaze Hazelwood unknowingly wound up on the set of a reality TV show.

This thrust the show back into the limelight, and for the past month executives at the Universal Products Company, the parent company of this network, have been working hard behind the scenes to have these stars return to Casa Grande. Now, finally, UPC is pleased to announce their new show: *Return to Casa Grande*. Here now to tell us about the show and to shed some light on their own stories is the cast."

The camera moved to the cast, who were arranged on a multilevel makeshift stage. In the center was Elizabeth Pierce, dressed in a smart navy-blue pantsuit and looking every bit the matriarch. Sitting down one step in front of her were the actors who played her children on the show, Vanessa Crestwood and Danny Maieye. Vanessa was dressed as the rebel, wearing jeans and a leather jacket; Danny was dressed more conservatively, in a black suit sans tie. Behind Elizabeth, one step up, were Victor Tillmans, who played the caretaker of the fictional vineyard where the show took place, and Blaze Hazelwood, who played the caretaker's son. Victor was wearing a plaid shirt and jeans, while Blaze had on a navy sports coat, white dress shirt, and designer jeans.

Kitty amazingly looked younger today than she did 25 years ago when *Casa Grande* went off the air. After numerous cosmetic surgeries to tighten her neck, raise her cheeks, lift her eyes, and repair what gravity was doing to her boobs, Kitty looked more like Meg Ryan in her *When Harry Met Sally* days than Meg Ryan did now! Her first question was directed to Elizabeth Pierce. "Elizabeth, you were a big star even before *Casa Grande*, having played leading lady to actors such as Rock Hudson and James Garner. What attracted a Hollywood starlet such as yourself to *Casa Grande*?"

"It actually almost didn't happen. I originally turned down the role, because I wanted to focus my energies on motion pictures rather than television."

"So what changed?" Kitty asked.

"I took a meeting with the show's creator, A. Michael Spaulding, and he convinced me that this role would not be the run of the mill damsel in distress role—that the character of Madeline Thornridge would be strong, cunning, and independent."

"And was she ever," Victor added. The cast showed their agreement with subtle laughter.

"That's a nice segue to you, Victor," Kitty said. "You were also a household name in 1980, when the show first aired—what attracted you to the set?"

"At the time, I was living in California and had a young family. I was tired of being away from my family, shooting movies on location. When I heard that the producers wanted me for *Casa Grande* and that the show would be shot in Southern California, it was a no-brainer."

"Vanessa, we practically watched you grow up on television; the show started when you were eight years old and ended when you were 18 and your character was very rebellious. Did life imitate art in your case?"

"Well, as many of you know, I was a bit of a wild child back then."

"I'll say," Danny said.

"It was the '80s and I was making a lot of money and had little to no parental guidance. In short, I had a blast." The studio audience laughed.

Kitty turned her attention to Danny. "Danny, you were no angel yourself back in those days."

"Back then, no one would use the name Danny Maieye and the word 'angel' in the same sentence! I was a hard-partying TV star who also toured in a rock band. But I am happy to report that those days are behind me."

"And now, to the man who made it all happen, Blaze Hazelwood. Blaze, did you know that the altercation you had with your neighbor that fateful night would lead to all of this?"

"I think it's fair to say that I had no idea anyone remembered our show. I am as surprised as anyone that it led to all of us getting together."

"I heard it took a little convincing to get you on board with the idea. Can you tell us a little more about that?"

"Well, I've been pretty vocal about my general disdain for reality TV, so when my agent pitched the idea to me I pretty much laughed in his face."

"What made you change your mind?"

"Well, for one thing, Allison Hart has a proven track record of success in this genre, so that was appealing. Also, the opportunity to reenact some of the classic *Casa Grande* scenes seemed like fun."

Kitty said, "You're referring to the aspect of the show where the cast is challenged to reenact a classic scene from the original show, and viewers at home get to vote on who did the best job. At the end of the season the cast member with the most votes wins a sponsorship contract for a UPC brand."

"That's right," Blaze said. "I think it will be a blast to relive some of those classic moments."

"All of you have gone your separate ways since the show ended. What have each of you been doing up until now?"

"Well, I escaped from a retirement home," Victor offered.

"And I helped him," Danny offered.

"Ah, yes, Father Daniel came to my aid," Victor added.

"What do you mean, 'Father Daniel'?" Kitty asked.

Vanessa was quick to respond, "This former Hollywood bad boy found Jesus and became a Catholic priest about ten years ago."

"I had no idea," Kitty proclaimed. "I don't see a Roman collar on you, though?"

Elizabeth, who had been silent for too long, chimed in, "He probably left it on the floor of the confessional when he was being serviced by the choir director." The Johnny Walker had apparently started to kick in and her lips were becoming looser.

"That's not what happened!" Danny protested.

"Wait, you had an affair with a choir director? That sounds like a storyline from *Casa Grande*."

"I maintain my innocence!" Danny shouted.

"When are you just going to admit the truth, that you couldn't keep your little Saint Peter in your pants?" Elizabeth said with a giggle.

"It's not that little," Vanessa mumbled, loud enough to be picked up on her microphone.

Kitty could not pass up the opportunity to capitalize on what she just heard. "Vanessa, are you admitting to having an affair with Danny?"

"Affair?" Elizabeth blurted out. "Hell, she had his baby!"

"What?" Danny shouted.

"I wanted to tell you earlier, Danny, but I couldn't. When we were on that bender in Vegas, I got pregnant with your baby. When I found out you were joining the priesthood, I decided to keep it a secret and asked my sister to raise it."

"Sister? You never mentioned anything to me about a sister," Danny said.

Everyone on the set of *Morning Roast* was riveted by what was unfolding before them. While the segment only had 60 seconds left, the director and producers in the control room decided to run with it, as it was too good to cut. Allison, on the other hand, was mortified.

"Yes, I have a sister. I believe you know her."

"Who?"

Vanessa looked him in the eyes and said, "Kathleen Guilard."

Danny could not believe what he had just heard. "The choir director? It was you all along?"

"What am I missing here?" Blaze asked.

Elizabeth filled in the blanks for him, "Our little Vanessa got her sister to remove her clothing in a confessional and frame Danny—for revenge after he stranded her in a hotel room."

"As you can see," Victor said, trying to get the interview back on track, "there are a lot of interesting things you will all find out about as the show unfolds."

Elizabeth, who was visibly intoxicated by this point, turned her head back to Victor and said, "Do you like the taste of my cookie, Victor?"

After hearing these words, Victor stared blankly into space and then suddenly started to remove his clothing.

"Victor, what are you doing?" Blaze asked.

"I have to get out of here! I have to get out of here!" Victor shouted.

The director and producers were getting nervous about where this segment was heading, but they also knew they were witnessing TV gold, so they decided to keep the camera rolling, even with Victor half naked and roaming through the makeshift studio.

"Why don't you ask Blaze here what his motivations are for doing the show?" Elizabeth asked.

"Well, Blaze?" Kitty asked.

"I'm looking forward to working with my old friends and reliving some great memories."

"Bullshit," Elizabeth said, forgetting that she was live on network television and there were laws against profanity. "You are just sick and tired of being the voice of cartoons and video games. Just admit it."

"At least I was working, unlike all of you," Blaze retorted.

"Whatever you say, Christian Clay," Vanessa responded. "At least we stayed true to our craft; you, on the other hand, took any role you could get."

"'True to our craft'? You did a series of soft-core adult films after leaving the show! How did that work out for you, darling Vanessa?"

Elizabeth said, pointing at Blaze, "The truth is, you are sleeping with Allison Hart. I thought you only went for older women—to the day she died, Bea Arthur boasted to me how she took your virginity."

Kitty Carson's mouth dropped even wider. "I thought those were just rumors."

"No, they were true; I was there. Bea tried to convince both me and Rue McClanahan to join them, but even the actress who played that slut Blanche had standards."

Blaze, clearly mortified by the news, was about to

defend himself when an older man forced his way into the mansion from the outside patio door. Seconds later he had two security guys attached to him and his cries of "Noooooooooo" could be heard throughout the studio.

The director said, "Keep the camera on the intruder and tell security to let up on him. Let's see where this takes us."

#

Don Carboni had watched his daughter's interview outside on the patio and he was absolutely beside himself; he had not seen his son in nearly 40 years, and now there were only some 25 feet and a door separating them. Don's heart leapt for joy at the sight of his son.

The boy Don raised as Bobby Carboni had changed his name to Blaze Hazelwood after being moved to California by his mother. Don had always dreamed that Bobby and his mother would come to their senses and come back to life on the farm, but it never happened. Within a few months of moving to California, his son had landed a few commercials, and soon after that he graduated to playing bit parts—Don watching all along. But *Casa Grande* was the show that changed his son's life forever. The rest of America watched with Don as a young Blaze Hazelwood went from cute pre-teen to handsome heartthrob in the span of 10 years. For Don, the most painful thing about *Casa Grande* was watching his son perform on television the job he should have had in real life: that of a farmhand.

Don watched the interview attentively. It began harmlessly enough, with the interviewer exploring the cast and their motivations for reuniting. But one minute the cast was talking about the show and the next they were pointing fingers at one another. Don grew agitated by all the fingers pointed at his son, and when he noticed a production assistant coming out onto the patio, he inched his way inside.

When he heard Elizabeth accuse Blaze of sleeping with Allison, he stopped walking and ran onto the makeshift set.

#

"Noooooooo! It can't be!"

If the cameras had been pointed at Allison and Blaze they would have captured them mouthing "Dad?" at the same time. But they were all pointed at the screaming intruder.

"There is something strange going on here in the studio," Kitty Carson said. "Apparently a crazy man has made his way into the building."

Blaze left his spot on the stage and walked towards his father. He was unaware of Allison doing the exact same thing.

"Does anyone know who this man is?" one of the security guards asked.

In unison, both Blaze and Allison said, "He's my father."

If a camera had been pointed on Kitty Carson, it would have shown her mouth drop open. For once in her life, she was speechless.

In the control room the director spoke into his microphone, "Are you getting all of this?"

Each of the three cameramen replied in the affirmative, now pointing their cameras toward Blaze, Allison, and the man who had burst onto the set from the outside.

"Your father?" Allison asked Blaze.

"Yes, my father," Blaze said to Allison.

"That's impossible," replied Allison.

"Why's that?" asked Blaze.

"Because he's my father!"

"Get a close-up on the father," the director said into his microphone.

Everyone in the studio, including Elizabeth Pierce, who was legally inebriated, was silent.

"Allison," Don began, "before I married your mother, I was married to another woman."

"I knew that you were married," Allison said. "But you never said anything about having a son."

"Because at that time I believed I didn't have a son anymore. In an effort to escape life on our farm, my first wife ran off with Bobby, who you know as Blaze, and took him to Hollywood."

"That's a lie!" Blaze protested. "She told me you were having an affair."

"When the hell did I have time for an affair? I worked on a farm from sunup to sundown, and every other waking minute was spent with you. Your mother was too ambitious for farm life and you were her ticket out."

"Come to think of it, I do see a resemblance," Vanessa whispered to Danny.

Danny whispered back, "This is kind of like how in *Return of the Jedi* we find out that Luke and Leia are twins separated at birth."

"There is something more that I need to tell you," Don said. "You are not just brother and sister—you are twins!"

At that announcement, Elizabeth Pierce literally fell out

of her chair, and Danny whispered to Vanessa, "I called it."

"I am fifteen years older than she is," Blaze said. "How the hell could we be twins?"

Don described how Blaze had been conceived through IVF and how a leftover embryo had been implanted in Allison's mother years later.

"Is it true?" Don asked with fear in his voice. "Are you two having an affair?"

"No," both Blaze and Allison said in unison.

Blaze continued, "From the moment I saw her, I felt as if we had something in common, but I couldn't explain it."

Allison thought of the bag she had packed just a few days before, intent to stay at Blaze's place after visiting the *Casa Grande* set. She silently thanked Catherine Philips for interrupting what would have been a very unfortunate event.

"Oh, thank Christ."

"Please refrain from taking the name of the Lord in vain," said Danny.

With all of the excitement around Blaze, Allison, and their father, no one noticed that Victor had now stripped completely naked and was headed out the door that led to the patio.

Blaze saw him first. "Someone give me a coat, quickly."

Don, Allison, a security guard, and a cameraman followed them outside to the patio.

CHAPTER FORTY-FOUR
Who Stabbed Kyle Dixon

Catherine Philips was standing on the patio in a disguise: a wig, dark sunglasses, and a trench coat. Ever since she was a teenager, she'd dreamed of the day she and Blaze would profess their love for each other, but that dream ended when Blaze chose Allison over her. While she was somewhat aware of a commotion going on in the mansion, she was so focused on getting revenge that she wasn't paying attention to the drama unfolding nearby.

Her trance was broken when the door opened and a naked man walked out. Right behind him was Blaze Hazelwood, and Catherine rushed toward him; as she ran, she removed her disguise.

In the control room the director once again spoke into his microphone, "Please tell me you are getting all of this on camera."

Blaze was too slow to react and Catherine knocked him over. Fortunately for Blaze, he was quick to get on back his feet.

"I thought you were in a loony bin somewhere in

Arizona."

"There is no room secure enough that can keep me from you, Blaze. We are meant to be together, why can't you see that?"

Security was at the ready to take Catherine down but the director in the control room was telling them to stand down. He wanted to milk this for all it was worth. "Wait to move in until someone's life is in danger, otherwise keep a safe distance. This is pure morning gold."

"Catherine," Allison said, "Can't you see he doesn't want anything to do with you?"

Inside the mansion, Kitty Carson was pressing a finger into her earpiece. She nodded a few times and then looked into the camera, "We've just received word that the woman on the patio is a bigwig at the Universal Products Company. A source tells me that she has been infatuated with Blaze since she was a teenager."

"Catherine, you are not well," Blaze said. Come inside and let's sit down and talk this out."

Catherine started laughing maniacally. "Talk, Blaze, that's all we ever do is talk. I need something more."

"Well you are not going to get it from me, luv," Blaze said with his British affectation.

That was the straw that broke the camel's back. Catherine reached into her coat pocket and pulled out a knife.

From the control room the director shouted his instructions, "Do not move in yet, let's see where this takes us."

Catherine then pronounced, "For twenty-five years we've wondered who stabbed Kyle Dixon! Well, today you will all get the answer. It was me—I stabbed Kyle Dixon!"

Catherine rushed toward Blaze and knocked him down for a second time. This time, however, she sat astride him.

Straddling him, she stabbed him in the right side of his chest. The security team, disobeying orders from the director, swooped in and pulled Catherine off of Blaze. Moments later, the patio was swarming with security guards. Minutes later, an ambulance arrived and rushed Blaze to General Hospital as officers handcuffed Catherine and took her away.

Kitty Carson looked directly into the camera and said, "I honestly didn't think there would ever be a show that could capture elements of suspense, intrigue, and revenge quite like *Casa Grande* did in the '80s. This just goes to show that sometimes the truth is stranger than fiction—you just can't make this shit up!"

Epilogue

January 29, 2016
Return to Casa Grande?
by Kitty Carson
(Reprinted with permission from *The Soapdish*)

I have covered soap operas since their earliest days on television. It's fair to say that I have seen it all. However, no fictional storyline that I have ever followed was as wild as what unfolded last week amongst the cast of *Casa Grande*.

It seemed like a good idea—capitalize on the newfound nostalgia for all things '80s by building a reality show around the cast of one of the era's best-loved shows—but unfortunately, tensions were too high, memories were too long, and jealousy was too rampant. After last week's debacle on national TV, the sponsor for the show, an unnamed Universal Products Company brand, decided that the cast was too controversial and that it would soil the reputation of a well-loved brand. I believe they made the right decision.

Not only did Allison Hart receive the shock of her life

by finding out she'd almost had a fling with her twin brother, but she was fired immediately from her position at UPC. However, my inside sources tell me that this decision was quickly reversed for reasons that were not made public. Rumor has it, though, Allison is in possession of a very steamy video that could bring down a major player at UPC, and this was almost certainly a factor in the reversal of her firing.

Danny Maieye received a call from the Archbishop of Los Angeles, formally apologizing for the way his case was handled. Danny was offered to be reinstated as a priest at Our Lady of the Hills, but he declined and instead accepted an opportunity to star in a reality show with Vanessa Crestwood and their son, Alan Michael. The show will be called *My Secret Family* and will begin airing over the summer; Allison Hart is set to produce, and it will be filmed in the *Casa Grande* mansion in Malibu.

John Lennon sang "Instant karma's gonna get you," and that's just what happened to Monsignor Paul Allen, who had it out for former *Casa Grande* star Danny Maieye. Apparently, one night some neighbors had been complaining about a loud party at the Our Lady of the Hills rectory and the police were called to check things out. The door was opened by a man dressed in drag, who immediately screamed, "Five-Oh, code blue." The policemen then forced their way inside and found Monsignor Paul Allen in the basement in the middle of what appeared to be a sophisticated chemistry set. It turns out he was cooking meth and was known to many in the greater meth community as Monsignor Meth. He was arraigned on charges related to operating a meth lab and, since no one posted a bond for his bail, he's getting a glimpse of what life in LA County lockup is like.

One of the strangest things that happened last week was Victor Tillmans stripping his clothes off in the middle of the *Morning Roast* interview. His former retirement home reports that this happened to him from time to time, typically after receiving a phone call from Elizabeth Pierce. It turns out that Elizabeth had hypnotized him years ago and planted a suggestion that he would go into a trance and strip after hearing her say the phrase, "Do you like the taste of my cookie, Victor?" She's now in a rehabilitation program for alcohol dependency, and Victor has decided to move back into his retirement home, where he can lead a more normal life.

After watching how Hollywood had affected the five stars of *Casa Grande*, Thaddeus Stevens decided to drop the T-Bang persona altogether and started applying to four-year colleges; his plan right now is to go pre-med. Eventually he'd like to be a pediatrician.

Catherine Philips was initially charged with the attempted murder of Blaze Hazelwood after her insane stabbing on the patio of the mansion. Since then, doctors have determined that she was not in her right mind; she has been sentenced to 1,000 hours of community service and is currently on paid leave from her job at UPC. She and her husband, UPC CEO Brian Philips, are now legally separated.

Stanley Roth, agent to the *Casa Grande* stars, was devastated at how *Return to Casa Grande* ended, because he knew he was going to miss out on a major commission. But no one was more surprised than he when calls started coming in for Blaze Hazelwood. It seems as if Blaze's brush with incest and his admittance of losing his virginity to Bea Arthur made him that much more interesting to the people who work in Hollywood. Stanley, it seemed, would not have to worry about money for a long time.

Which brings us to Blaze Hazelwood. What can I say— this guy has nine lives. Nothing bad ever seems to stick to him. Blaze has had his pick of projects roll in, and my sources tell me he has decided to play the lead character in a show called *Mike Slammer*, a parody of *Mike Hammer*, a popular '80s television series starring Stacy Keach. Blaze will play the title character, who is hired by older women to investigate whether or not their husbands are having an affair. Invariably, this leads to Blaze sleeping with his clients, and the show is built around the complications that arise afterward—another case of art imitating life.

I think it is safe to say that the curtains are now closed on Casa Grande for good. Perhaps this lesson has taught us that there can be too much of a good thing and that the past should stay in the past. Or maybe this is a lesson about how forgiveness, understanding, and selflessness are the traits we should live by. But then again, who am I kidding? This is Hollywood, and we don't encourage such behaviors.

Acknowledgements

The character of Blaze Hazelwood was born on a car trip to Philadelphia, and he could not have been conceived without the collaboration of my good friend and trusted ally Joe Indusi. We were somewhere in New Jersey when we started speaking in British accents and trading off grandiose statements just to pass the time ("I once starred in Back to the Future the musical"). I named my character Blaze Hazelwood and we decided that we should create a universe in which Blaze and his friends could live. We decided it would be fun if he was an aging actor trying to find relevance in the era of reality TV, and the idea for Return to Casa Grande was born. Joe has served as a great sounding board for this story and I am indebted to him for his collaboration and direction.

My friend Oonagh Petrizzi read the first version of Return to Casa Grande and provided me not only with encouragement for the story but also a tremendous amount of direction on how to improve the writing. Thank you, Oonagh!

I am also indebted to another editor, Eagle from Aquila Editing who provided invaluable feedback on this story and helped make me a better writer in the process. Thank you, Eagle, even if you didn't get all the '80s references scattered throughout these pages.

I cannot forget to thank my longtime friend Jacqueline Burt Cote whose advice and encouragement kept me going through multiple revisions of this manuscript—hair metal still rules.

Erin Wathen and Lisa Ferraro were the first of my friends to finish the revised version of Return to Casa Grande, and their advice, direction, and encouragement served to improve the story and make it funnier in the process. Thank you, Erin and Lisa.

I must say that this book would not have been possible had I not known my maternal grandmother, Maria Fauci, who religiously watched soap operas on CBS. Unlike other boys my age, I didn't come home from school and head to soccer or football practice—I sat down with my grandmother and watched The Bold and the Beautiful, As the World Turns, and Guiding Light. Viewers of those soaps may see some familiar names and faces in Return to Casa Grande.

Made in the USA
Columbia, SC
02 July 2018